Books by William Price Fox

Southern Fried Plus Six
Moonshine Light, Moonshine Bright
Doctor Golf
Ruby Red
Dixiana Moon
Chitlin Strut and Other Madrigals

CHITLIN STRUT
& OTHER MADRIGALS

WILLIAM PRICE FOX

Illustrations by Jack Davis

PEACHTREE PUBLISHERS, LTD.

Published by
PEACHTREE PUBLISHERS, LTD.
494 Armour Circle, N. E.
Atlanta, Georgia 30324

Manufactured in the United States of America

Library of Congress Catalog Number 83-61916

ISBN: 0-931948-46-0

For
Sarah and Kathy and Colin
with love

Contents

The Chitlin Strut

N OW, FRIENDS, I have seen dancing. I was there when Chubby Checker opened it up at the Peppermint Lounge in New York City, and I've seen them pick them up and lay them down at Small's in Harlem, and I was there with Satchel Paige in Kansas City when a six-foot-two mocha beauty did a concentrated version of the Dog up on a table top that I have indelibly engraved on my brain and would like carved on my stone. I have also seen the belles of Southern Bell and the wipers, sweepers, weavers, and the girls from the loom room of the cotton mills in Columbia do a profane version of the Hully Gully that there's a sherriff's order out against. But when I saw Jack West of Landrum, South Carolina, lock down on the Chitlin Strut, all I can say is what two drunks in front kept saying over and over and over again . . . "Now that's what I call dancing. Now *that's* what I call dancing."

But first a little background: In 1966, Mayor Jack Able of Salley, South Carolina, (population five hundred and fifty) decided his town needed money for new Christmas decorations, and so the first Chitlin Strut was organized. A curious one thousand showed up, ate (or didn't eat) the chitlins, did the Strut, and went home and told their friends. The word spread. People came from Charleston, up from Hell Hole Swamp and Moncks Corner, and down from Columbia and Greenville. Seventeen years and seventeen Struts later, sixty thousand tickets were sold and five tons of chitlins were scraped, braided, boiled, battered, deep-fat fried, and served.

Some Low Country, nineteenth-century historian is credited with the phrase "a chitlin is better discussed than described." Anatomically, they are the intestines of the hog, and normally are used as sausage casings and ground up into lunch meats and hot dogs. But for a fried chitlin you must, as the saying goes, "go whole hog." The chitlin, a long tube-like affair, is stretched out and scraped down, then turned inside out and scraped again. Three lengths are braided together, boiled until tender, then battered, deep-fried, and served.

And who will eat a chitlin? Max Gergel, a Columbia sage I travel with and who is famous for promoting the now defunct insecticide "Sam Chewnings' Roach's Last Supper" (featuring a four-color label of twelve roaches chowing down at the da Vinci table), explained: "You take a man and tie him to a stake and feed him bread and water and nothing else for seven days and seven nights, and then he will eat a chitlin." Max, who can stretch and roll a sentence out until it sounds like it was lifted from Ecclesiastes, paused carefully. "He won't like it, but he will eat it."

The Chitlin Strut is held in late November, when the weather's cool and the breeze is up. One old-time cook: "Lord, we'd never cook them things here in the summertime. That smell would kill every green thing growing." During the "boil down," no buzzards circle Salley and no jackals stalk the live oaks and the scrub pine. Small dogs

whine and cringe and large ones head for the corn and the
bean rows to escape the suffocating stench that hangs in the
air impenetrable, undissolved, incredible. An outsider:
"Lord, how do y'all stand it?" The cook: "You get so you get
used to it. Go sit in the car and turn the air conditioner on.
You don't look too good."

The year was 1971, the sixth Chitlin Strut. Despite four
inches of gray, cold rain, twelve thousand people showed
up to eat and dance. The long line for hot, fried chitlins
snaked around the Crescent City Vocational School eaves
out of the driving rain, down the long main corridor and
into the serving area. Armed with deep draw, latch-lidded
styrofoam trays full of chitlins, cole slaw, rice, and biscuits,
the customers headed for the gymnasium bleachers, the
corridors, and the small classrooms. In the machine shop
they hunched over their hot meals on the South Bend lathes
and the long-shafted drill presses. Outside the rain was
breaking all records for western Carolina, and the
passengerless Ferris wheel looked like a Misissippi riverboat against the low gray sky as it caught water on its slow
circle up and poured it out coming down. The cotton
candy, the Pronto Pup, and the foot-long chili dog
concessions were out of business. Only the snake show, with
the aid of one hundred yards of thick polyethelene
strategically draped to protect the crowd and a low wood
fire smoldering away to keep the snakes warm, made it. The
owner, hatless, with water dripping from his nose and ears
and plastering his black hair flat, explained how South
Carolina was number one in the nation in poisonous snakes,
nosing Florida out by seven to six. He counted on his
fingers, showing how both Florida and South Carolina have
the exotic coral snake but only South Carolina has the
dreaded timber rattler. A local nodded at the sleeping boa
constrictor and announced that he had it on authority that

the snake doesn't actually strangle a man. He went on to explain that the snake's method of operation was to wrap himself around a man, wait for him to exhale, and then take up the slack. The owner, slicking the water from his face, went about his business and held up the fourteen-pound timber rattler to a twelve-year-old girl wearing a Chitlin Strut beanie.

"Mister, I know snakes, and I just don't believe I can go along on that one."

The girl was curling her lip, and he pulled the rattler back, asking if she were scared.

She frowned; "Ain't you going to milk it?"

He said he would, and, squeezing the fangs against a metal fork into a small shot glass, he held up the yellow venom. She beamed. "That's the part I like best."

In the combination auditorium-gymnasium — a 1910 low-ceilinged, tall-windowed, red brick building where bad music sounds terrible and good music sounds great, with a raised stage on one end and the basketball nets pulleyed up to the ceiling — the action started. A local group of musicians, after ten minutes of tuning up and then giving up, were trying for the audience's sympathy with an old bleeder, "I'm Using My Bible for a Road Map." In the third row a steel guitar player, in tight Western black jeans with scalloped pockets studded with rubies, green stones, and yellow matching his guitar case, was chewing chitlins and complaining about the low quality of the lead singer.

"That equipment's worth two thousand dollars and will you listen at that *sound!* The only thing that dude's got going for him in Ohm's Law."

His neighbor was wiping down grease. "This is a tough room to work. Look how everybody's moving around and talking so."

The steel man with sideburns like pocket combs and creases that came with three counts of murder snorted,

"Rough! Hell, I played in places with no windows, no chairs, nothing. You couldn't even get a *can*, much less a bottle, of beer. Everything served in Dixie cups . . . and you talk about fights!"

"Where'd the band sit?"

"Squatted, friend. That place was *rough*."

Between the chitlin eaters on the first row and the stage, the first dancer came forward. At forty he was in red double-knits, a white plastic belt, and glistening white vinyl boots complete with metal heel and toe plates. His hair was pumped up and he wore it in a fast-back Billy Graham duck swoop, which he whipped and molded into shape with a sixteen-inch comb that was also white. In his head he was Fred Astaire, and when he made his long swooping shuffles and glides across the base line, he machine-gunned his taps like castanets. His eyes were fixed on the middle distance for isolation and concentration, but during the richer mixes and fast banjo work, he hairpinned down to study and marvel at his flying feet.

Two hairdressers, a mother and daughter combination, dressed in matching tight-fitting blue pantsuits that had turned purple in the strange rain-filtered light, joined him but wouldn't let him cut in. During "Your Cheating Heart," they broke into a 1950 Lindy. The mother stayed out on the long break with her eyes closed, her face soft, feeling the words behind the words or remembering some red-rimmed neon honky-tonk, some old and long-gone love. The daughter finally brought her in. The song moved from blue to bluer and the tap dancer's face went from pain, to earnest, to tender. Then chording an invisible guitar, he lightfingered the phantom frets and strings and serenaded the hairdressers and the first row with Merle Haggard's "It Ain't Love But It Ain't Bad."

Max and I were sitting in the bleachers. I was eating my chitlins and asking about the length, scope, and various duties of the hog's lower intestines. Max chewed his cole slaw slowly.

"I'd say there is very little, if any, of the hog of today that's thrown away. But you could throw a polecat into five-hundred-fifty-degree deep fat and get by with it, if you served it fast. Besides, if you get a hungry man half drunk, and after all that dancing, that fool's eating anything smoking. Grease — that's the ticket." He swallowed the cole slaw and, dodging the chitlins, went for the biscuits.

"Grease — that's the secret of the South. This is the hard lard belt down in here. You go in a store and ask for something like sayflower oil and they'll think you're part of the Red Menace."

A strange cross-bred Dalmation was crawling on his elbows under the seats, opening the styrofoam trays, eating the leftover chitlins, the biscuits, the rice, the slaw.

On stage the band, getting little resistance from the audience, had faded into their theme and rolled their amplifiers to the wings. A new group plugged in and quickly tuned into a wild upbeat version of "I Got 20/20 Vision But I'm Walking Around Blind." An electric shock rippled the crowd. The new sound filled the room, the hallways, the machine shop, and they began moving. Suddenly the first three rows of folding chairs had been knocked down and dragged away. The room was warming up, the steam had fogged the windows white. They were dancing in the center aisle, on the sides, and out beyond the free-throw line. The low ceiling held the music tight and the chitlin eaters were hog-calling, swamp-shouting, stomping their feet and screaming for more.

A short, hairy man, half drunk and red-eyed and wearing a baseball cap and gas station whites, was trying to move in on the mother and the daughter, but they were having no part of him. The music kept building. The dancers surged forward; whole rows rose as one. Men danced alone, women alone, men together, women together, two four-year-old twins were jogging in place, and a clutch of teenyboppers in tight jeans and braless body shirts were mincing up and down the galleries delivering the mail to the driving beat of J. D. McIver and His Starbusters from Columbia. They came from every corner of the room, each with his own moves, his own vision: pumphandles, eyes-closed dreamers, feet-watchers, rubbers, dippers, sliders, tango-swoopers, and fast-break soloists, who'd hunch back down on their hands in some double-jointed trash dance and hootch until the embarrassed girl would scoot for the cover of the crowd.

The Dalmation was under the tenth row and working his way to the rear, leaving a trail of empty trays behind. And then it happened. Someone had arrived. They were turning around, straining to see him.

"Who is it?"

Someone shouted, "It's Jack! Jack West!"

They were standing on their seats to see him.

"I'll be damned. It's him all right."

An old-timer dressed in bib overalls, drinking white whiskey out of a Dr. Pepper bottle and gumming a biscuit, slapped his fifteen-year-old son on the back.

"By God, we'll see some dancing now. I knew he'd be here!"

J. D. McIver up on the stage saw him and went into a hyped-up version of "Won't You Be My Salty Dog," and Jack West came sliding through the chairs sideways, grinning to his friends and fans and out into the center aisle. Jack was short, fat, and when he grinned he looked like a baby hippo with his bright teeth, gleaming eyes, and shining pelt. He was coming forward dancing. The band moved in tighter on the mikes, the dobro growled lower, the fiddle went to the top of the neck, and the banjo went crazy as the bass pulled it together and locked it down so he could grab it by the neck. And Jack did. Unlike dances which can be done in small areas between cocktail tables and waitresses on sunken rug-sized floors, the Chitlin Strut requires room, lots of room. Jack came on shimmying like a '54 Ford with a bad front end, grinning and popping his hands on the big backbeat. But the shimmy walk was just to get there. There was more. The red double-knit tap dancer and the mother and daughter and the others peeled off and hung their elbows on the stage like they were watching a dogfight. The hairy drunk in the baseball cap, the gallery-walking teenyboppers, even the small kids, stopped. The room stopped. It was J. D. McIver and his Starbusters and Jack West. He took the center of the basketball key and the pool cleared, for he could hold it by himself. Jack West was dancing, and I closed the lid on my chitlins.

The band had shoved the amplifiers to the fire wall and the banjo had passed the speed of sound. The audience were standing on their seats, the kids were hanging from the window jambs, and every face and every eye was on Jack West. He went into a back bend doing a voodoo-limbo number with his belly while he grinned from ear to ear and flailed his hands like fan blades. Then switching quickly, he turned his back and, grinning over his shoulder at the crowd, he rolled it, twisted it, wound it up and let it fly, establishing one immutable law of the Chitlin Strut: It is not a thin man's dance. It requires bulk, displacement, a stomach and a rear view of hips, loins, and other choice cuts that a thin man cannot provide. West cranked it up faster and faster, locking himself to the driving beat, and moved into a rag-doll-and-bugaloo throwaway, heading for his big move. The fiddles were squwaunking at high C and higher with lightning work up on the neck; the dobro was filling the gym, and the amplified bass was making the basketball rings vibrate and the steamed windows hum in their casements. Jack made his move. Faster, stronger, wilder, longer, mad, crazed, seized. He was on the fine point, just this side of an epileptic fit that would cut in and plunge him into convulsions, terminal tremors, and madness.

The crowd: "You sure he's all right? Looks like he's been taken hold of."

"Jack's fine. You ain't seen nothing yet."

"You're kidding."

He wasn't. For Jack, in the middle of what had to be a spasm, suddenly increased the voltage and, spinning quickly on one hand, vaulted up over the plastic rhododendron and the stage lights. He was up on the stage grinning down. The band was with him, now closer, tighter, wilder. They peaked and leveled for a second to get directions on a bridge and began building again.

"Jesus, where's he going *now*? Will you *study those feet!*"

"Is he drunk?"

"No, just happy. Man, all we have is fun back up in them mountains."

He spun again, dropped to one knee, then the other, and bounced up into a frenzied heel dance. The old-timer wiped his mouth from a long pull on the Dr. Pepper bottle and shouted, "Hogback Mountain Clog! Right, Jack?"

Jack grinned and nodded.

"He's been drinking that steam whiskey."

"Naw, I came down with him. He ain't had a drop yet. Hell, I've seen him get out of his car with the radio on and just dance out in the road right in the middle of town. Happy bastard, ain't he?"

"Right! Get her Jack! Whip it boy! Hook 'em! Hook 'em, boy!"

Jack passed the point of spasm and, in the frenzy and the froth you see only in the back of salvation tents and Pentacostal jubilees, he held his shaking hips and loins to the incredible beat for another thirty-six blistering bars. Then he screamed and leaped back over the plants and stage lights to the middle of the free-throw zone.

He went back farther, and, looking up to where the moon

would be if it were dark and clear, he cut loose with the only Southern finish possible — the long, dark, subterranean, unmistakable deep-swamp sound of a Carolina redbone who has treed a twenty-pound possum or a forty-pound cat. The old-timer who had called the clog hooked his head and joined in. He changed keys and, baying down deeper and drawing it out like he'd picked up a fresher trail, a stronger trail, he popped his son on the back with one hand and raised his white whiskey to the ceiling with the other. And then catching his breath, he shouted to the bleacher-stacked, whistling, screaming pack of eaters, dreamers, watchers, dancers, "By God, now that's what I call *The Chitlin Strut.*"

Doug Broome, Hamburger King

O UT UNDER THE red and green and the yellow fast-food neon that circles Columbia, like Mexican ball fringe, Doug Broome was always famous. As an eight-year-old curb hop, he carried a pair of pliers for turning down the edges of license plates on the non-tipping cars; he was already planning ahead. He grew up during the Depression in the kerosene-lit bottom one block from the cotton mill and two from the State Penitentiary. When he was nine, his father went out for a loaf of bread and, in storybook fashion, returned eighteen years later. Doug left school in the fourth grade, worked his way up from curb boy at the Pig Trail Inn out on the Broad River Road, to Baker's on Main Street, and finally to his own restaurants all over town.

There was a "Doug's" on Lady Street and, while I was still in junior high, he hired me on the sandwich board and the big grill. He taught me how to stay on the duckboards to keep from getting shin splints, how to make an omelet, and a hundred things behind the counter that made life easier. I copied his freewheeling moves with the spatula and the French knife, his chopping technique on onions, and his big takeaway when he sliced a grilled cheese or buttered toast. He also introduced a lot of us to the ten-hour day, the twelve-hour split shift, and the killer twenty-four hour roll-over. Somehow he thought we all had his energy.

Doug Broome had energy, incredible energy. It may be the kind you see in skinny kids playing tag in a rainstorm or the stuff that comes with Holy Roller madness. He had black curly hair, bright blue eyes, wore outrageous clothes, and every year had the first strawberry Cadillac convertible in Columbia. When he was young he won the jitterbug contests all over town, taking shots at everything Gene Kelly was doing in the movies. He was wild with clothes. With cars. With women. Some of his checks may still be bouncing. To investors coming to town on business with him, Doug was a mystery, a threat. His pink-piped matching shirt and slacks and his lightning ways with money scared them off. To them, a bounced check or a bankruptcy judgment or a stack of subpoenas was like the neck bell and the tin plate of the leper, but in Doug's empire this was only his way of doing business. And Doug had an empire. He became the father he never had for his family, his help, and his friends. He worked them, loved them, punished them. Sometimes he would sit down and list the problems he was having with them. Someone was getting married before they were divorced, or divorced without benefit of attorney. Some couple would leave for a Stone Mountain honeymoon with the back seat stacked to the window level with Doug's beer and the trunk loaded down with Virginia hams and cigarettes. Someone was always running off with a friend's wife or husband, getting drunk, wrecking the wrong car, and getting locked up. And a few of the more spectacular cases managed to do everything at once.

Doug would just grin and say, "We're just one great big

old family out here, mashing out hamburgers and making friends." When they were in jail, Doug bailed them out. When drunk, sobered them up, and when in trouble or sick, he gave them his lawyer and his doctor. He never took them off the payroll. They stole a little, but Doug with some sixth sense knew about how much and made them work longer hours. It was a good relationship, and when the unions came around to organize, Doug's people would just laugh and say they'd already been organized.

One day he told me, "Billy, these chain operations are ruining the hamburger. Ruining it. Most of them come from up north to begin with, so what in the hell they know about cooking? Any fool right off the street will tell you the minute you freeze hamburger you ain't got nothing. God Almighty, you slide one of those three-ouncers out of a bun and throw it across the room and it *will sail*. I ain't lying, that's how thin that thing is." He was eating his own Doug Broome Doubleburger. "Now you take this half-pound baby. I don't care what you think you could do to it, there ain't no way in the world you can make it any better. No way. I use the finest ground meat there is. The finest lettuce, the finest tomatoes, and onions, and Billy, I fry this piece of meat in the finest grease money can buy. These chains are getting their meat up out of Mexico. Ain't no telling what's in it. Hell, I read that in a government magazine."

He went on about how he had gunned down the "Big Boy" franchise when it rolled into South Carolina. "Everybody in town knows I've always called my hamburger, 'Big Boy.' You used to serve them. Am I right or am I wrong?" He didn't wait for an answer. "Anyhow, they'd already steamrolled across everything west of the goddamn Mississippi. And here they come heading across Tennessee. Then across Alabama. Then across Georgia. But when they hit that South Carolina line, I said 'Whoa now! You ain't

franchising no Big Boy in here because I am already the
Big Boy. Gentlemen, you and me are going to the courts.'
And that's what we did. They brought in a wheelbarrow of
money and eight or nine Harvard Jew lawyers, and all I had
going for me was my good name. And Billy, we beat them to
death. I mean to death. They had to pay me sixty thousand
dollars, all the court costs, and everything." He paused and
sipped his coffee. "Well, you know I never like to kick a man
when he's down, and those boys had all that money tied up
in promos and 'Big Boy' neon, so I say 'Okay, y'all give me
another ten thousand dollars and you can have the
franchise, and I'll change my "Big Boy" to "Big Joy." ' "
    I knew a few of the facts. "Come on, Doug."
    And then he raised his hand to Heaven.
    "Boy, why would I tell a lie about something like that?"
    Part of the story was true. Outside on North Main the old
"Big Boy" read "Big Joy." But the eight or nine Harvard
lawyers turned out to be one old retainer out of Charlotte.
The sixty thousand dollars was right, but it went the other
way; Doug had been the infringer and had to pay them.
The ten thousand dollars never existed. Doug was like that.
Like all great storytellers, he was a consummate liar. A
straight tale would be transformed into a richer, wilder
mixture, and the final version, while sometimes spellbind-
ing and always logical, would have absolutely nothing to do
with the truth.
    But I remember one crazy night on Harden Street. We
were in the kitchen. It was July. It was hot. Oral Roberts was
in town. He was still lean and hungry and doing Pentacostal
tent shows. "No! I'm not going to heal you! Jesus is! Jesus
Christ is going to heal you! So I want you to place both
hands on your television set. And I want you to pray along
with me. And if you ain't got a television set, place your
hands on your radio. And if you ain't got a radio, any
electrical appliance will do."

At the air-conditioned eight-thousand-seat tent, it had been standing-room-only, and every soaring soul had descended on Doug's for hamburgers, barbecues, steak sandwiches, fries, and onion rings. Doug and I were on the big grill, the broilers, the Fryolaters. Lonnie was on the fountain. Betty Jean, under a foot-high, silver-tinted beehive, was on the counter and the cash register. The parking lot was jammed and another hundred cars were cruising in an Apache circle looking for a slot. In the kitchen the grease was so thick we had to salt down the duckboards to keep from slipping. The heat was a hundred and twenty degrees and rising. The grill was full. The broilers were full. There was no more room. There was no more time. We had lost track of what was going out and what was coming in. Horns were blowing. Lights were flashing. The curb girls and Betty Jean were pounding on the swinging doors, screaming for hamburgers, barbecues, steak sandwiches, anything. And then suddenly there was another problem. A bigger problem. The revivalists were tipping with religious tracts and pewter coins stamped with scriptural quotations.

The girls were furious. "One of them gave me a goddamn apple! Look! Look at it!"

And what did Doug Broome do? I'll tell you what he did. He stripped off his apron and pulled Betty Jean out from behind the counter. Then he triggered "The Honeydripper" on the juke. No one could believe what Doug was doing. He was dancing and Betty Jean was doing red-hot little solo kicks on his breaks. When the song ended, he announced that everyone was getting a twenty-five dollar bonus for working the Pentacostals, who had scriptural support for their stand on no-tipping. Then Doug flipped on the public address system and sang out over the cars and the neon and the night, "Ladies and gentlemen and boys and girls, I'd like to take this opportunity to remind you that you are now eating at one of the most famous drive-ins in the great Southeast. Our specialties are hamburgers, barbecues, and our famous steak sandwich, which is served with lettuce and tomato, carrot curls, pickle chips, and a side of fries, all for the price of one-dollar-and-forty-nine-cents. And when you get home tonight and tell your friends about our fine food and fast service, please don't forget to mention that we have been internationally recognized by none other than Mister Duncan Hines himself. . . . I thank you." Then tying on his apron and angling his cap, he came back to the grill and with some newer, faster, wilder speed I'd never seen, he caught the crest and broke it.

Doug had style, but it wasn't until years later that I realized what a profound effect it had on me. I was on a New York talk show hustling a novel. The host had led me down the garden path in the warm-up, promising we'd discuss pole beans and the price of cotton. But when the camera light came on, his voice dropped into low and meaningful. We discussed the Mythic South, the Gothic South, Faulkner's South, and the relevance of the agrarian metaphor. I was a complete disaster. All I wanted was out. And then he asked how I would define style. It was a high pitch right across the letters, and I dug in and took a full cut. I told him about one day during a lunch rush at Doug's on Harden Street. There had been a dozen customers on the horseshoe counter and a man came in and ordered a cheese omelet. I'd never made one before, but I'd watched Doug do it. I chopped the cheese, broke three eggs into a shake can, added milk, and hung it on the mixer. Then I poured it out on the big grill. I'd used too much milk and it shot out to the four corners getting ready to burn there in twenty seconds. I almost panicked. Then I remembered Doug's long, smooth moves with the spatulas and pulled them out of the rack like Smith and Wesson .44s. I began rounding it up.

As I worked, I flexed my elbows and dipped my knees and did a little two-beat rhythm behind my teeth. I kept singing, kept moving, and just at the crical moment I folded it over, tucked it in, and slid it onto the plate. Then with parsley bouquets on the ends, and toast points down the sides, I served it with one of Doug's long flourishes and stepped back.

The man forked off an end cut. He chewed it slowly and closed his eyes in concentration. Then he laid his fork down, and with both hands on the counter, he looked me in the eye. "Young man," he said, "that's the finest omelet I've ever put in my mouth."

I wound up telling the stunned interviewer that *that* was style, and all you can do is point at it when you see it winging by and maybe listen for the ricochet. I don't think he understood, but I knew I did. I knew that style wasn't an exclusive property in the aristocracy of the arts. A jockey, a shortstop, a used-car salesman, or even a mechanic grinding valves can have it, and the feather-trimmed hookers working the curbs along Gervais and Millwood are not without it. But Doug Broome not only had it, he knew he had it, and he staged it with wild clothes and great music, and he backlighted it with red and yellow and purple flashing neon.

Well, Doug's gone now, and with him goes his high-pitched voice on the p.a. and the nights and the music and the great curb girls out on Harden Street who got us all in trouble. He's gone and with him go those irreplaceable primary parts of Columbia that shimmered out there under the cartoon-colored neon. There will be no buildings or interstate cut-offs named for him, nor will there be a chandeliered Doug Broome Room at The Summit Club. But some nights out on North Main or Harden or Rosewood, when the moon's right and the neon's right, and a juke box is thumping out some sixties jump or Fats

Domino is up on "Blueberry Hill," it will be impossible not to see him sliding doubleburgers and Sunday beers in milkshake cups down the counter. And if you're as lucky as a lot of us who knew him, you'll probably see him pinch the curb girl at the pick-up window and give her that big smile and say, "Baby Doll, remember there's no such thing as a small Coke."

The Fish Fry

I T WAS A simple plan. A heroic plan. A stupid plan. Jeff and I would pay the full four hundred dollars and rent a charter out of Murrell's Inlet, catch a swordfish, filet it up into a hundred steaks, and bring it back to Columbia for a fish fry. At 3:00 A.M. we were eating bacon and eggs and grits with a side of hot biscuits and raspberry jam, and by 4:00 when it was still dark, we were out on the black Atlantic heading for the Gulf Stream, where the marlin and the big swords play. While the captain had told us to prepare for a long day, he didn't tell us to eat a very light and very dry breakfast. Fifteen minutes out in the rising and falling swells, we were hooked over the low rail with the bacon and eggs, the grits, the biscuits, the jam. While Jeff was sick, I kept assuring the captain all was well. When I was sick, Jeff said the same for me. When we were both sick, he stopped asking. Eventually we sat back, glassy-eyed and exhausted, waiting for our strength to make a move. At some magic moment, the captain opened two beers for us. It tasted wonderful and not only cooled the fever, it soothed the pain. Another beer later and we were crazily planning a commercial where two fools like us are out on a charter boat sick and dying. At the last minute, in strides red-white-and-blue Captain Beer, who saves the day and our four hundred dollars, and we wind up with a five-hundred-pound swordfish and our pictures in the national press.

Pelicans and gulls were winging in ahead of us, heading for the fresh food of the Gulf Stream, and directly in front was an orange-red sun so soft you could see the rim and pick out the leaping fires. We arrived, baited the big hooks, and sat back, bracing ourselves in the fighting seats, waiting for the shock of the marlin, the sword, the shark.

Out in the Gulf Stream it's hotter, over a hundred; the water is greener, and clumps of fern and kelp and whole stalks of palm trees from all over the South Seas come drifting by. That was all that drifted by. For the eight solid hours we trolled and drank beer and ate peanut butter sandwiches and rubbed in suntan oil, we didn't see a single fish — not a single mackeral, not a single mullet. Finally the captain cleared his throat. "Well, boys, it looks like this just ain't your day. They were hitting everything yesterday."

On the long trip back into the setting sun and then the darkness, Jeff, hunched over a matchbook cover, figured that the sixteen beers had cost us twenty dollars apiece, the eight peanut butter sandwiches only ten dollars.

Late that night, sunburned and beaten down, we debated forgetting the fish fry and heading on back home. But then a new plan surfaced; we could back down from swordfish steaks to pompano, which is a delicious eating fish, or perch, or bass, or whiting. We could go out on the party boat that the big sign at the dock was proudly advertising:

WE GUARANTEE — YOU WILL CATCH FISH!
OR YOUR MONEY BACK!

At eight the next morning, we paid our fare and climbed on board the party boat. We were given a rod and a reel, hooks and lead, a bucket to keep the bait in, and a plastic basket for the fish. The captain, on a p.a. system high above us in an off-limits cabin, welcomed us on board, and we headed out the channel. In the trade, party boats are called "head boats" (twenty dollars and thirty dollars a head). Ours was a big iron monster stretching out eighty or ninety feet with metal tubes every eighteen inches for holding our rods. Standing there shoulder to shoulder, the one hundred and thirty of us looked as if we were chained together on a slave ship bound out for some exotic Dutch possession. One bass boat whined by, and the owner actually swiveled his seat around and turned his back on us. And on out in the channel, an angry housewife screamed and shook her fist as our big wake rocked her pier and almost rolled her boat. No one waves at a party boat.

At nine the sun was high and hot and the metal rails were heating up. Next to us a couple from Greenville were having a hard, hard time. The wife, tall and pretty with a spaghetti halter, went pale, then paler, then green. She eased down slowly on the bench, covering her eyes and whimpering about the seven-and-a-half hours that lay ahead. The husband soon followed. He was big and tough and determined to ride it out. He did. He fished, threw up, and kept on fishing. Their friends kept laughing. "We told y'all not to eat those hush puppies. Ain't nothing but solid grease."

"Leave me alone."

"And you didn't shut up till five. What in the hell you expect?"

"I didn't expect this."

The wife finally sat up but kept her eyes closed against the blinding glare. "Paying all this money just to lay here. Lord!"

The fish were biting — perch, sailor's choice, black bass — and all around was the sound of beer cans popping. An attractive Charleston woman with blue-rinsed hair was looking over the shirtless beer drinkers and the retchers hooked over the rail with true disappointment. "I must say, I never expected this. I thought it was going to be a party boat. You know, deck chairs and waiters running around serving Bloody Marys. Some party."

Two old pros in jump suits and green-striped Adidas shoes reeled in black bass and sailor's choice. As Jeff battled a Michelin whitewall radial to a standstill before the bait boy cut him off, I hooked onto a four-foot shark. He took off under the boat in a great swoop, gathering up twenty to thirty lines. Then when he had all he could reach, with a single shake, he threw the hook and went on about his business. The tangle took fifteen minutes to unravel.

Of all the fishing boats that smoke out of Murrell's Inlet, the bottom of the line is the party boat. But in the great pecking order of things, there is always someone lower. Party boat sports reserve their contempt for the landlocked men and women who fish from the piers. I once heard a dishwasher in his kitchen whites put down the mop boy. His withering logic was that someone could mistake him for a doctor, while the mop boy would be forever linked to his mops and wringer bucket. It is to these gossamer sails that we press our dreams. Party boat fishermen reason that since they throw their fish back in, they are sport fishing. Pier fishermen keep everything. Down here in the Low Country, he is known as a "meat fisherman." When we steamed back in by the collection of men, women, kids, and dogs fishing from the pier, one fellow in an orange jumpsuit with tiny zippered pockets in his lapels shook his head. "Jesus, look at them. That's where I draw the line." His sidekick, in the same suit but in phosphorescent green, was greasing down his neck from a raging sunburn. He closed his eyes and winced, "I just couldn't live like that."

That night Jeff and I had another meeting and decided to forget pompano and now concentrate on perch and spots. They are smaller, easily cleaned and, when fried right in fresh grease, delicious. We would risk scorn and fish from the pier.

In the morning, with our hands stamped PAID, we set out for the end of the eight-hundred-and-fifty-foot Surfside Pier. For four dollars we had rented a rod and a reel and enough squid to fish all day. Pier fishing is by far the cheapest; it is also the easiest. Instead of a metal tube, we had benches with canted boards to rest our arms and rods on. Next to us was a sink with running water to clean fish, and above were lights in case we decided to stay all night. Across the aisle a mother and a father were pulling in spots and sailor's choices while their four kids, all under six, were crouched in over Red Rock strawberry drinks and Moon Pies. The mother rebaited her hook. "Rhett, you're the oldest; don't let them bolt that stuff down like that."

"Yessum. Can we have some money for the Ferris wheel?"

"No! And will you stop pestering me!"

They had brought along coolers of cold drinks and beer and enough sandwiches to keep the kids busy. The coolers, which the kids were rapidly emptying, would go home with twenty, thirty, or even fifty pounds of fresh fish. It's a long day, and the family had brought along a radio to listen to the World 600 and the baseball game. Out on the end, the overnighters came equipped with chaise lounges, blankets, tape decks, and battery-powered coffee makers. They, too, were plugged in to hear how Richard Petty and the brothers Allison were running. Unlike the party boat, which goes out twenty to thirty miles, and the marlin boats' sixty and seventy, the pier is right on the bank. Many people fish two or three hours, then have someone watch their poles while they go see a movie, have a steak, or cruise up to Myrtle Beach to "Ripley's Believe It or Not." Benches run down the middle, and the old-timers are staked out here, giving out information about the winds and the tides and identifying the strange creatures drawn up from the bottom. Surfside Pier is full of surprise catches, and before noon four sandsharks and two hammerheads had been hauled in, along with a couple hundred blowfish and a sheepshead the size of a good-sized Labrador. The outstanding record here was set in 1962, when George Singleton pulled in a hundred-and-twenty-eight-pound tarpon. The fish, in all its former glory, is still hanging in Lee's, a glassed-in restaurant on the land end of the pier. George, an affable real estate drummer, says he fought the fish for more than three hours with half of Surfside looking over his shoulder. Finally he tired him out and walked him down the pier and brought him out on the beach. The soles of George's shoes had sweated through, and he says that even today when he thinks about the struggle, he gets a pain in his back.

Jeff and I pulled in hand-sized spots and perch until our arms were weary. Our spirits were up; our sink was filling fast. To us, pier fishing was superior to party-boat fishing and marlin fishing, and after a few beers we were calling it "The Sport of Kings." We began adding names to our guest list. Maybe we'd serve French fries. Hush puppies. Maybe both.

Unlike the party boat or the charter boat, no one on the pier was sick. There is no roll. One old Valdosta boy, overcome by Yarborough's loss at Charlotte, drank too much and went to sleep at his post. Someone wound in his line and tied it off for him. Two more sharks were pulled in, and a twelve-year-old girl from Macon reeled in a twenty-pound white bass. Jeff and I were figuring on about two pounds of fish per person and had the guest list up to forty. It was going to be a great night; all we had to do was clean them and cook them.

Cooking fish, unlike catching them, is simple. You scale

it, clean it, load it down with cracker crumbs, and lay it gently in five-hundred-and-fifty-degree grease. You turn it once. Down here in the hard-lard belt, we eat everything — the tail, the dorsal fin, the mouth, head, eyes, and all. The cats, returning to some ancient savagery, dispose of the darker organs, then calm down to clean and polish the bones. And since any walking hound prefers fish bones to pork chop bones, the rest goes out on the step for Old Trailer and his youngest son, Boomer. In short, the fish, like the hog and the Great Plains buffalo, is ecologically perfect; there is no waste. Fish scales are scalloped around the "God Bless Our Mortgaged Home" signs and, in the hands of a proper artist, gilded gold and magenta to liven up the sea shell memorabilia that crowd the mantles from Cocoa Beach to the Great Barrier Reef. But first you have to clean them.

It is the problem that comes to all fishermen. Jeff and his buddy Randy a year before had caught an eighty-six pound amberjack. The amberjack is famous for his many bones and his rapid decomposition. He can't be eaten; no one wants him stuffed. All he is is big. They waited until the dead of night, dressed him in a hat, necktie, plaid sports coat, and sunglasses, then slid him down the lawn of a friend's house, where he came to rest at the bottom step. The friend, in turn, waited for the next night and levered him into a Dempsey Dumpster in back of the K-Mart. In the morning, the police arrived with the sheriff and the press. Meanwhile, downwind, some suffering citizen had called the coroner.

Jeff and I bought a cooler and some ice and two sharp knives. I made the first incision. Suddenly all the beer, the sickness, the sun, and the rhythm of the Gulf Stream came rolling back. I told Jeff I couldn't do it. He said he couldn't either and didn't want to see another fish. A kid who had been hanging around made us an offer we couldn't refuse.

He would do it all for five dollars. We made the deal.

The kid had his own special knife and went to work fast. He was thin and barefooted and looked like the original Tiny Tim. Finally we decided that he needed the protein more than us. His parents would be grateful. They, in turn, would pass this good deed on to some other needy family, and on down the road the world would be a better place in which to live. I drank another beer, feeling mellow, benevolent, expansive. Maybe I'd go to church Sunday. Send a check to the Red Cross. Be a better husband, a more understanding father. Maybe I'd even bring the family down to the pier. The kid thanked us three or four times, then asked if he could borrow the cooler. Jeff put his hand on the thin shoulder. "Tell you what, son. You keep it."

We had decided to have an old-fashioned barbecue instead of an old-fashioned fish fry. The kid thanked us both again. Then, stepping down the pier, he unashamedly pulled out a pocket scale and began weighing and selling them off for a dollar a pound. In five minutes he made fifty-six dollars. Then turning around, and with the empty cooler under his arm, he winked once and went whistling down the pier. Later, an old salt told us that he did that every day, and every day some sap fell for it. So if you're ever down at the Surfside Pier, this kid is about five-feet-one. He's barefooted, has blond hair and pale eyes. Jeff and I figure he's a lot older than he looks.

The Drive-In

B ACK IN THE fifties, I worked out at the Starlite. I took the tickets and popped the corn. I hung the speakers, cleaned off the graffiti, and tapped my flashlight on the fenders of the lovers whose heads had dropped below the window level. "O.K., back row for that! Back row!" On the men's room walls it usually ran, "Gertrude does it, Edith won't. Mable can't."

In the women's it was more explicit. We used to say, "Lord, that's nasty."

When I returned not so long ago, Dewey Corbin was running my old Starlite. Dewey, a religious man who helped out in church work and Little League, didn't show X-rated films and was careful with the Rs. He charged three dollars a car for *Gentle Ben,* and no one had to hide in the trunk or down on the floorboards. In front of his panoramic screen, children played on the swing set and the slides, in the sandbox and the pool. In the wintertime the pool was filled with hay. Dewey had decided that rather than have the kids sneak in over the fence, or under it, he'd let them in free to sit up front and help with the baby-sitting. These kids grew up loyal to Dewey; they made sure nothing got too wild or out of hand at the Starlite.

Dewey walked me through the concession stand. My old phone-booth-size popcorn stand had been stretched out sixty feet and handled Pronto Pups, hamburgers, French fries, cold drinks, and ice cream. The counter help was uniformed, trimmed and polished, and looked as if they'd done time down at Disney World. Outside, the old ramps and speaker stations and guide lights looked the same. Dewey said, "I guess it hasn't changed too much. Same old rules. No lights on the screen. And if you want to make out, go to the back row. If I see the heads going down, I kick them out. We keep it a family operation."

At the new Starlite, it seemed, the only change since I worked there was the hardware and the price of popcorn. But then, as the sound track came crackling in over the speakers, I wondered if the crowd had changed, and if so, who would know.

In Charlotte, there was Bob McClure, who, as they say in the trade, "knows it from its inception." He produced *Preacherman* and *Hot Summer in Barefoot County.* McClure, a soft-spoken snappy dresser, had his walls covered with eight-by-tens of Tarzan and Jane, Clark Gable and James Cagney, and featured in the center was a big one-sheet of Tom Mix riding through 1935 with the Texas Rangers. On his desk was a bottle of Scotch, a bottle of vodka, a king-size Gatorade, and a poster of his newest release.

We talked about the early drive-in days. "Hell, it started right around here. All of it. I got a buddy who booked them." He telephoned Hugh Sykes, who said he would be right over, and I eased in front of the Gatorade and headed for the Scotch.

Hugh Sykes drank his vodka straight, wore French slacks, and flew his own airplane. He jiggled his Gucci loafers like expensive daggers as he and McClure went back over the forties, trying to pin down where the first feature flickered out over the first cow pasture. The story goes that an enterprising farmer set up two telephone poles and a screen in a flat field and, with a movie and a projector, went into business and launched an era. Much conversation passed as to whether it was a cow pasture in South Carolina or a bean field in North Carolina. The consensus seemed to be toward the beans. What the movie was is lost back there in the Carolina dust, but Sykes remembered that the farmer had charged twenty-five cents a carload and had set up a "foghorn-blast speaker" at the side of the screen.

McClure remembered the crowd. "See, this was way before TV came along, and those old farm boys would watch anything moving. Anything. They'd come right in in the middle of the story, and it wouldn't matter a bit. And then a lot of kids came out on the field and got in behind the cars and lay out there on blankets and watched it. See, it was a novelty and, of course, everyone wanted to see who all was out there. I guess at first it was probably more like a social occasion than anything else."

Sykes talked about the commerce. "You could rent a movie for twelve dollars a week. So after your first fifty cars or so, you were into straight profit. Those monkeys made money. Big money."

They talked on, about how the first owners sunk decoy poles to let everyone think they were planning to open up a second place to keep the competition down, about the first angled ramps and the early speakers, and how boiled peanuts were the first item at the concession stands because no one had a popcorn machine. And then, sliding along through the forties, they talked about some long-forgotten night when Tex Ritter, with no stage to work from, hunched down over his guitar and played *Rye Whiskey and Boll Weevil* up on top of the concession stand. As they talked on, I couldn't help thinking about what a fine night it must have been back there lying out under the stars in that first field, eating peanuts and watching all this and wondering where it was all going.

* * *

"Starlite, starbrite . . . Lord, don't let it rain tonight." At the drive-ins across the country, they all agree on one thing: If you're going to show an Ingmar Bergman Festival, do it in the rain. Out under the stars, you will find no retrospectives of Einstein or salutes to Fellini. *Citizen Kane,* with a personal appearance of Mister Welles himself, would languish, but anything that Elvis touched will run forever. There are all kinds of promotions to bring the cars in; an Easter Eve show will run *The Robe, The Sign of the Cross,* and end at dawn with *The Ten Commandments* and a forty-foot cross against the screen, and the local minister asking for flashing lights and horns for those who love the Lord. A Halloween show might go all out and give away a free coffin, a cemetery plot, and a free funeral. A triple-feature, Laugh-O-Rama, lucky-number holder might take home a year's subscription of Kentucky Fried Chicken and a trunk load of brand-name chickpeas. They have tried, and are trying still, train rides and pony rides, beauty shops and barber shops, bingo, laundromats, car washes, merry-go-rounds, and swimming pools.

Promoter Terry Holman was famous for his giveaway of a dead body during a five-feature Horrorthon. It was a frozen turkey. He ran a four-hundred-fifty car capacity setup eight miles out from Columbia. It had air conditioning units equipped with window gaskets that kept the mosquitoes out, and a transmitter system where you could dial the sound track on your car radio; if you had stereo, so much the better. Holman's location was perfect, with tall trees for a road screen on one side and a truck stop on the other. The drivers parked their trailers and drove over in

the tractors. With their diesel stacks, the rigs were over
twelve feet high, and Holman made them park at the back.
"My biggest problem isn't good movies, it's vandalism,"
he said. "I lost three air-conditioning units in one month.
Those things weigh damn near a hundred pounds. Hell,
they'll steal anything, steal the speakers and take them over
to Georgia and sell them to another drive-in."

Holman, an enterprising promoter, not only sold beer
cheaper than the bars in town, but he also supplied the
county with most of its X-rated soft porns. Down here
where the "Jesus Saves" signs are thicker than rednecks at a
white-sock sale, the fundamentalists and the pornogra-
phers have arm-wrestled to a draw. In the men's rooms,
Bible-college students still Scotch-tape pictures of Jesus
over the vending machines for PROLONG and DELAY.
But for Holman there was no problem. "The Pentacostals
will line up for Pat Boone's *The Cross and the Switchblade* and
anything with an Art Linkletter voice-over. But then there's
a lot of folks down here who would just as soon see what
Linda Lovelace is doing, too. You want to know the best
drive-in movie ever made? *Thunder Road.* Don't ask me why.
Maybe it's the chases, maybe it's Robert Mitchum. But it's a
doorbuster. I could bring it in tomorrow and I'd be
packed."

The last time he booked *Thunder Road,* he set up a
moonshine still with dry ice boiling up to look like it was
cooking, and a local deputy standing by to tell the people
about lead poisoning and the bacteriology of what happens
when small creatures of the night drop into the mash vats.

"It's all a matter of shekels. A good movie will bring in the
shekels, a bad one won't." He waved his hand disgustedly at
an old *Great Gatsby* poster on his wall. "A real turkey. Now
what I want to know is why in the hell a nice guy like that
who can make *Jeremiah Johnson* could get talked into doing a
loser like that. That really gets me."

Down here where the cottonmouth and the possum roam

and up to the soybean prairies around Des Moines, if a fan wants to sweat out the Pronto Pup line at the concession stand or move in on his girlfriend, he wants to be able to resurface into the simple plot he left behind. An angry drive-in crowd leaning on horns and flashing lights quickly gets the message back to the owner and the producers. Some say that this is the kind of feedback that brought Rome to its knees. But Terry Holman would argue that he was merely bringing the people what they wanted to see.

* * *

Across the border and up where the red clay gets redder, I asked a Georgia owner if he really bought the stolen speakers from the Carolina drive-ins.

"Hell, yeah. They buy ours. Friend, this is a very competitive business. Listen, you printing this?"

"I'd like to."

"Well, take my name and place off. I'm in the divorce courts right now, and we're getting ready to divide things up. I got to keep me a low profile."

"I'll call you Max and we'll move it close to Augusta."

"Fair enough."

Max under-belted his stomach low, and on his forearm was his wife's name tattooed in blue with a recently etched red line running through it. Popping open two beers, he slid me one and then, for absolutely no reason, launched into a monologue on the Great Depression. "I was in Savannah, Georgia, and I saw a wharf rat sitting on a garbage can eating an onion. Now a wharf rat is probably the smartest animal that travels on four feet. Friend, I want you to know that rat was crying real tears. That's how hard times were down here."

Max's office was built in behind his concession stand and, like Holman's and McClure's, his walls were lined with one-sheets and glossies. A small refrigerator was loaded down with six-packs of Miller High Life, and on the wall above it was a mica-flecked sign: BOWLING — A DRINKING MAN'S SPORT.

Max had been in the drive-in business since the early forties, and I asked him if the crowd had changed since then.

"Damn right. Sex is different now. Back in the forties and fifties, it was all rassling and steaming up the windows. Now they come out here with pillows and plug in eight-track stereos. Can't you see some old leather-backed greaser with a set of pillows?"

He popped a beer and watched the foam run. "I can look out some nights on my back row and I won't see a single head. Not one. Everybody's going at it. I could be running black leader. But I'll tell you something, we don't have any trouble out here. I mean none. Kids are more sophisticated."

I asked him if the older crowd was getting smarter, too.

He belched and headed for the refrigerator. "TV's changed them. It'll probably wind up burying them, though. They're all beginning to sound the same. But everything comes in waves. They build up, they top out, and then they drop. Beach-blanket stuff was hot for a while. Then it was Steve Reeves and the weight lifters. Now it looks like it's horror stuff and the occult. You got to keep stirring it up and trying something else, because nothing lasts. Nothing."

He smiled and polished up a line behind his eyes that he'd been saving. "If the price of gasoline keeps going up, we're going to be sucking wind out here in the turpentine. You know what I told an old boy one night? I said high-priced gas is going to do for the drive-in what panty hose has done for fingering." He leaned over to make sure I'd gotten it down right. Then he opened two more beers. "I been shoveling this crap to them for thirty years now. Sometimes, when I get drunk enough, I get a little sad about it all."

I checked his eyes to see if he was joking.

"I mean it. Friend, that crowd out there is the crowd that skinned through high school on C-minuses and Ds. They're still wearing their football sweaters. And I mean they don't read one book a year, any year. But all I got to do is remind myself of that rat eating that onion, and I get over it. People went hungry back then, and kids didn't have any shoes. Those people have come a long ways. Now days some old boy who's worked his ass off all week humping a pulpwood truck can look back in his station wagon and see his kids safe and sleeping, and he can open a cool one and maybe reach over and grab the old lady. When you stop and figure it out, we're giving them a helluva bargain. I don't give a damn what's up there on the screen. The kids are sharper, too. Fast. Fast as lightning. You know when they screw out there when we got a good show on? During the cartoon."

He got up and hitched his stomach around the edge of the desk and hollered out, "Alice!"

A voice came back. "She ain't here."

"How about Fern?"

"She's gone too."

Finally he called a girl in. "Jessica, come in here, honey."

She stood in the doorway with her hip sprung out. Her blouse was cut off at the second rib.

Max said, "Honey, you ain't wearing no bra under that thing."

"It's hot out there."

He introduced me and told her to tell us about an incident from the year before.

She started in about riding around one night and he stopped her. "No, that ain't it. The Camaro."

"Oh, that."

She spoke flat, as if giving directions to downtown Augusta. "We were doing it in this Camaro." She looked at me. "You know, screwing?"

I said I knew and asked, "Front seat?"

"Naw, you can't do it there. Anyhow, this acne case comes up and asks us if we wanted to buy some Girl Scout Cookies. Now talk about embarrassing. My boyfriend told the kid to come back later. And you know what that little shit did? He just hung there in the doorjamb and said he'd wait and see if he could learn something new. I mean, he wasn't even eleven years old."

As Jessica left, Max winked. "What'd I tell you. Want another beer?"

"Don't mind if I do."

The last show was over and the cars were leaving the lot when Max stripped the plastic from another six-pack. Max said, "They're smarter out there, more direct." And I agreed. In an indoor movie house, a bored customer will groan and twist in his seat and maybe bitch out in the lobby after the show is over. But out in the cars, out under the stars, drinking beer and eating chicken and making love, it's still a buyer's market, and it's different. Out here, they've been secure enough long enough to flash their lights and blow their horns and pound on the doors and hoods until the producers have finally had to give them exactly what they want.

Max said, "They ain't so shy anymore; now they're a pain in the ass." Then sitting back he watched a beetle circling the ceiling light and had the last word. "But you know, when you get old and fat and maybe have to go the aluminum walker route, this is the way to do it. I'll tell you the God's own truth. I'd rather see a movie in my Buick. Friend, I got me a little refrigerator in there, and talk about something that's convenient . . ."

Celebrity Golf

ROUTE 275 out of Harleyville is a two-lane blacktop winding through a part of South Carolina that may never change. "Impeach Earl Warren" has faded badly on the smooth rocks and run-off culverts, but "Get Us Out of the UN" is still with us in fresh spray paint, along with directions for night crawlers, she-crab soup, and head and root readings. One sign in tortured hand lettering outside Bluffton — the area that gave the world Father Devine, Reverend Ike, and Joe Foster — looked like it had been lifted from Guinness' Book of World Records: "Man has gotten away with more sin and unrighteousness during the past twenty years than during any period since God drove Adam and Eve from the Garden of Eden."

Traveling here through the possums (the small dog who does not bark) and the cottonmouths, it's best to keep the radio on country and western AM stations. The theory being that c/w cannot stand up under the scrutiny of FM-stereo. As the Hilton Head signs thickened, a preacher came on with a piercing nasal voice that made my treble speaker crackle. The signal was fading, so I stopped and popped open another beer. "Yessir! Yessir! We've had exorcisms out here! We had one last month. Little gal out near the K-Mart Mall was having a terrible time. Terrible! What she was doing was this. She'd run out behind the house and get out behind the barn and spin around three times and leap up in the air. And while she was up in the air she would disappear. You hear me! Disappear! And that wasn't all! She would reappear in a bar in downtown Savannah. Well folks, that kind of thing happens every week over in France and Germany and places like that, and they're used to it. But I'm telling you, that was new around here. But I got down on my knees and I stayed down on my knees praying until I got that little gal right through that thing." As he segued into a love offering pitch, I flipped to an FM station and headed out across the Jimmy Byrnes Memorial Bridge to Hilton Head, the island of the Mercedes and the BMWs.

In South Carolina, everything happens on Labor Day. The football season opens, the Darlington 500 revs up, and across the sandhills and the Piedmont and on down the Congaree and the Cooper rivers to Charleston, more than a hundred official barbecues, okra struts, catfish stomps, and demolition derbies are all going on at the same time. But the big one, where the stars of the movies and television and the world of sports are, is the Celebrity Golf Tournament for Muscular Dystrophy.

The cast of characters contained forty-four brand-name celebrities from New York, L.A., Nashville, and the National Football League, along with several omnipresent politicians. Also in attendance were the Marine Corps Brass Band from Parris Island, eight breathtaking Atlanta Falcon cheerleaders, a cast of twenty-five for a fashion review, and enough beer and wine and whiskey and shrimp and barbecue to make a Georgia golfer named Felix dressed in Izod shirt, Izod pants, Izod hat, and an Izod belt shake his head in awe and wonder. "This thing is *big*. Somebody had to *plan* this thing." His partner, with a green player's badge reading "Ross," had a brick-red face and a glass of bourbon. "Some of these boys are really famous. Wonder what they had to pay them to get them to come here?"

Felix and Ross were both eighteen handicappers from Valdosta, Georgia, in the food machinery business. Their celebrity preference for a playing partner skipped right over Hollywood, right over New York and Nashville, and ran straight into the heart of the National Football League: Johnny Unitas, Kyle Rote, Ken Burrow, Tommy Nobis. We had another round and Ross said his reason for coming to the Celebrity was very simple. "For five hundred dollars, we spend three nights on Hilton Head, we play three courses, get to meet the ball players, and go to three dinners. Then when we get home, we mark the whole thing off as a charity contribution." But Felix's face clouded. "That ain't all of it. I don't know what it is, but that sure as hell ain't all of it."

Along with the celebrities (who were given air fare and out-of-pocket expenses) and the five-hundred-dollar playing guests, there were others. Two girls wearing matching tan safari suits with blue epaulets and white spectator ID badges, Kim and Anne, were working the crowd for autographs. Claude, with his back to the bar, spotted them first. "Hey, look at that crew."

Felix checked them over for class and conformation. "They're too old for groupies. Too young for wives. Reckon they're hookers?"

"Naw, not enough makeup. God, they're knockouts."

The girls eased in closer, looking for gold celebrity badges and Hollywood faces. Claude came on strong. "Hello girls. Come on, we'll buy you a drink."

The quick one, Kim, spotted his green player's badge and

didn't waste any time. "Sure thing, cowboy. Nothing like a big spender at a free bar."

Claude winked. "That a gal. Y'all from Atlanta?"

"No, Greenville."

Anne showed us Telly Savalas' name scrawled under his picture in the Celebrity Book. "I just love Telly, and he was so nice and friendly, I couldn't believe it."

They had rated the celebrities from one to ten. There were only seven tens, all from Hollywood: Telly Savalas, David Huddleston, Joe Gallison, Norm Alden, Steve Carlson, Bob Ginty, and Bobby Quinn, the director of the "Tonight Show."

Songwriter Mickey Newbury joined us and we pitched in, helping them get Spanky McFarland and Dave Loggins. Mickey waved over two more; it was David Huddleston, the mayor in *Blazing Saddles*, and Kenny Davis, the Vegas-Dallas comic. David and Kenny vamped over arm in arm, imitating all-star drag queens. David's limp wrist fluttered. "Dahling, I'm wearing my off-the-shoulder green tonight. And it's *sequins, sequins, sequins*." Kenny shimmered and batted his eyes. "They always love you. I'm the one they *hate*. Well, I'll show them. I'm wearing my muumuu and my Frye boots."

David signed Glenda's book "For Glenda, remembering that wonderful night on Pismo Beach."

Kenny won Kim's heart with "I'll Love You a Thousand Ways, Slim Whitman." The drag queens did a rhumba bump and glided off, and Claude pointed Kim at Bobby Riggs. "Now there's the guy you want to get. Couple years from now, that autograph will be worth some money."

But they had spotted Joe Gallison heading over and weren't listening. "Oh, Lord, he's beautiful. I didn't know he was that tall," Kim said. "I just love that smile." Joe Gallison, from "Days of Our Lives" and "Another World," with his gold celebrity badge shining brightly, had someone on his arm. It was his tall and beautiful and gold celebrity-badged wife, Melissa. Later Kim said, "I wish everyone that's cute and interesting wouldn't always bring their old wives along. It just isn't right."

Ross and Felix had missed the cut with the girls, but Newbury and I, with our gold celebrity badges, still had an outside chance. As we helped them sign up Fred De Cordova, the producer of the "Tonight Show," and Fred Holliday, the game show announcer who is famous for his straight man to Johnny Carson's Ronald Reagan, we saw the scores on the leader board. Cordova and Holliday were nines; we were down as twos. Kim said, "I'm sorry, but we just haven't ever heard of y'all. Either one."

Mickey said it reminded him of a "gal telling her husband to forget it" song, with a withering refrain that ran:

"I've gone and told the children you were dead.
I've even had a funeral for your side of the bed."

Mickey smiled, "Can't you squeeze out a three or a four?"
"Sure thing, hon. Y'all are kinda cute.
Mickey said, "There's Jose Ferrar. You want him?"
Kim's dark eyes darkened. "What's he do?"
"Cyrano de Bergerac. Remember that one?"
Anne cocked her head. "That wine commercial? I thought that big old heavy fellow did that one. You know, old what's-his-name?"
Kim snapped, "Anne, for God's sake, it's a movie." Jose Ferrar signed up.

Still later, when about a dozen of us were sitting around the pool watching an orange-red moon rising and the lights from Savannah twinkling out over the water, Anne began talking. She and Kim had switched from Pina Coladas to Scotch and water and finally to white wine. Anne told how they had both gone to the same high school and junior college together and were even married in the same year.

How they had wonderful husbands and children and two cars and Beta Maxes and circle driveways and how happy they were. . . . "But last year we got to drinking and we got to thinking out at the country club, and we decided that there was something missing in our lives." She started giggling and Kim took over without missing a beat.

"We decided that before our next birthday, we were going to come out here to the Celebrity and we were going to spend the night with a movie star. Now you talk about something crazy."

Next morning the tournament started in earnest. The Atlanta Falcon cheerleaders were everywhere: driving the carts, serving the beer and sandwiches, and posing for a picture with anyone carrying a golf club. The tournament couldn't have been held without them. The first two courses we played, Shipyard and Palmetto Dunes, like the cheerleaders, were long and lush and beautiful, and a great time was had by all. The last round was Harbourtown, the site of the annual Heritage, and the sixteenth, seventeenth, and eighteenth holes here, with the Sea Pine Lighthouse and the porpoises, the shrimp boats and the killer whales in the distance, may very well be the most spectacular finish in the country.

When the tournament was over and the awards were distributed, it was "all out" entertainment. Archie Campbell from "Hee Haw" did his barnyard version of Cinderella, Jimmy Weldom his voice of "Webster Webfoot," the Marine Band played "Stars and Stripes Forever," and the fashion review, to the themes of "Goldfinger" and "Chariots of Fire," wheeled and whirled over the plumed and lighted stage with the latest fashions from Gucci, Pucci, Ralph Lauren, and Oscar de la Renta. And then came the music.

Newbury, who wrote Elvis's "American Trilogy," Kenny Rogers' "Just Dropped In to See What Condition My Condition Was In," Ray Charles' "Sweet Memories," and

Jerry Lee Lewis' "She Even Woke Me Up to Say Goodbye," among others, did two songs beautifully and sat down. The next singer, Dave Loggins, came on and didn't sit down. He played the song he had written for The Masters, which CBS played over the Augusta, Georgia, event. One thirty-four-word line, sounding as if it had been lifted from Howard Cosell, recalled how Gene Sarazan won the tournament in 1937 with a double eagle on the fifteenth. The song was a long monologue, and the back rows began stealing away. One wag at our table said it was longer than "The Day the Good Ship Edmund Fitzgerald Went Down," but shorter than *Piers Plowman.* After two more numbers, he introduced Gove Scrivenor, a good-looking bearded type with an autoharp. He announced that he had written "The Twin Rivers" while he was living in Montana with his close friend Tom McQuane. He explained that if we closed our eyes and listened close, we would be able to see the rippling water and the mists on the forests and the mountains in the distance. The autoharp has a beautiful tone and Scrivenor was right; you could see the rippling water. You could see the mists rising in the climax forest and the mountains in the distance. You could almost see Tom McQuane. By this time, the back rows were completely empty and the tables around us were trying out one-liners:

"For an encore he's doing the complete works of James Fenimore Cooper."

David Huddleston grumbled, "My foot's asleep, and I envy it."

Kenny Davis added, "He's been on longer than I've been away from home."

But the best one came out of the shadows. "That back row moved to the bar faster than Charles Colson went to Jesus."

It was after the party, it was late, and everything was finally winding down. We were back out by the pool, with the moon back-lighting the palm trees and shining on the sands of Calibogue Sound. Anne and Kim were there; the Hollywood and Vegas tens and nines had let them down, but when they told us they had spent the night watching the Late Late, they began giggling and couldn't stop.

At first it was jokes: old jokes, new jokes, clean jokes, blue. Then football.

We moved on to golf: to the courses, the tournaments, the players. It was Jack Nicklaus, Tom Watson, Arnold Palmer, and back to Snead and Hogan and Nelson. Then someone raised the ante and said that tennis has ruined more marriages than golf. "I play with the old lady for an hour, and the only time I get to myself is when I go to the john."

Another voice. "Makes sense. Figure it this way: We're playing four, five, six hours at a crack. When we finish, we have a couple beers and head home. You hang around a tennis court with all those hard bodies out there and all you get is horny. No offense, girls, but that's the way I see it."

Anne said, "Yeah, I've got that, but what I want to know is why you have to come all the way down here to little old South Carolina. I mean, y'all are busy, or you're supposed to be. Why do you come three thousand miles just to play here?"

There were a dozen answers. It was like being back at the Y-Camp sitting around the fire and comparing DiMaggio to Mantle, to Williams, and telling about what we were going to be when we grew up.

One TV personality who had registered a seven on the girls' hit parade was quite eloquent. "You know, gang, if I had to tell you about my second wife, I could probably do two minutes before I ran out of material. But I can remember a two-iron shot I hit on the seventeenth at Pebble three years ago. I can tell you exactly how that ball left the club face, how it faded, and how it feathered up there four feet from the stick. Right now, all I have to do is close my eyes, and I can actually see the configuration of the clouds in the background. The reason I'm here, ladies and gentlemen, is golf." Then he spelled it out slowly: G . . . O . . . L . . . F. . . . ." Everyone was silent for a moment, thinking he was going to continue, but he didn't.

And then Felix stepped forward. He had reached his limit on Jim Beams and had eased into the beer. He popped open a can and cleared his throat. "They took a shot of us a while ago, me and old Boom-Boom Geoffrion and Kyle Rote and Willie Mosconi. See, I had my arms around the cheerleaders, you know, Mary Ellen and Cynthia and Arlene, and the guys had their arms around us. Anyhow, we were all standing there grinning and cutting up, and right there it hit me why I'll be back here next year. I mean, it stood out like a shotgun blast at midnight. Being here with you guys is, well, it's like being in the middle of a Miller beer commercial. Ain't that something?" He hooked his head and laughed. "I guess we're all crazy. Right?"

Anne hugged him and kissed his cheek. "Yea, you're all crazy. Every damn one of you. But you know something? I think you're all just as cute as you can be." She and Kim had a quick huddle and she announced, "I'll tell you what we're going to do. We're going to make all you fellows honorary tens."

And Kim added quickly, "For next year."

Whatever Happened to 'Chinese' Baker?

RIGHT UP front I'm saying that ninety percent of your so-called reading public thinks the best place for *The Enquirer* is on the hook in some Mississippi outhouse. See, they figure every story is going to be "Killer Dogs Invade East Bronx Nursing Home," or how the UFOs are landing and setting up housekeeping out on Pismo Beach. Well buddy, let me tell you something — that first page is there for the street-stand sales and the blue-rinse set at the checkout counter. You open it up and check out our in-depth stuff, and I guarantee you're going to be in for a surprise. My name's McCoy, Ed McCoy, and I've been on the Chicago staff for eight years, and I'm here to tell you that this is the best damn paper in the business. All they want is a good, fast-moving story and they do not, underline that, they *do not* mess with your copy. Anyhow, when I saw the Associated Press bulletin about a chimpanzee playing nose guard against Notre Dame, all I had to do was catch a plane, because that story was mine.

Like I said, A.P. ran the first notice: "Dateline, South

Bend, Ind. Oklahoma A&T shocks gridiron world by playing two-hundred-pound chimpanzee at nose guard in defeating Fighting Irish 10-7. Owing to the alertness of the CBS cameramen, TV viewers over the nation were able to see 'Jerry Jones' the chimpanzee in action. During the pandemonium following a brilliant last-minute goal line stand by A&T, where Jerry was credited with three unassisted sacks that saved the game, the chimp, caught up in the enthusiasm, grabbed cheerleader Amy Richards, 'The Golden Girl,' and carried her up the goalposts. Ms. Richards, who was unharmed, later admitted she enjoyed the attention. Further details are sketchy and contradictory at this moment, as Coach 'Chinese' Baker and officials at Oklahoma A&T have been unavailable for comment."

That nine minutes of footage of Jerry up on the crossbar with the Golden Girl ran everything off the tube. And I mean everything: national, locals, Canadian, PTL — hell, even the Mexicans couldn't get enough of it. Neilsen reported it beat out twenty years of "I Love Lucy" and was moving up fast on old Jack Ruby putting the move on Lee Harvey Oswald. There were double-page spreads in *People* and *Newsweek*, and *Esquire* had a cover showing Amy Richards in her skintight spangles, holding up Jerry's special pants and his special gloves and shoes. If you follow *The Midnight Enquirer*, you've got to remember my four-color centerpiece spread. In case you don't, on one side was the A.P. shot of Jerry with the Golden Girl slung over his shoulder up on the crossbar. I had DeAngelo paint in some vines and leaves and made it look like Jerry was taking her off to his jungle home to do the dark deed. On the other side, I had three tight shots of Amy crying and saying, "He's like all the rest . . . he doesn't write . . . he doesn't phone . . . he didn't even send me flowers." Now don't get me wrong — this Amy Richards is no fool. She came out of this as Miss January Playboy with a trip to

Hollywood and an open-end contract with the William Morris Agency.

Two weeks after my spread, an ape specialist out of Yerkes in Atlanta was on "60 Minutes" explaining that Jerry was a McHenry-Chow chimpanzee from Tasmania. McHenry is for O. L. McHenry, the guy that discovered him back in 1909. Chow is because of its bright red coloring and long hair. Well, with no one able to find Jerry or Chinese Baker, and the officials at Oklahoma A&T not even answering the phone, the story tailed off and finally died.

And then nine months later — WHAM! The wire service had it first. " 'Chinese' Baker, controversial ape coach from Oklahoma A&T, chokes to death at Palms Restaurant in midtown Manhattan. Close friends who were with him reported that a piece of New York strip steak had lodged in his throat and he did not respond to the in-house Heimlich's Choking Relief Procedure. Baker, 52, born in Atlanta, Georgia, played for Alabama for three years and was twice named to the A.P. All-American Squad. He later went on to the Coaching Hall of Fame while leading Oklahoma A&T to a total of two hundred and ten wins against sixty defeats and twelve ties. Baker will be buried in 'Coach's Corner' at Woodlawn Cemetery, Bronx, New York. Friends wishing to send flowers are directed to send contributions instead to the Football Hall of Fame, Canton, Ohio."

Well, I read this over about nine times, and then about nine more — because, you see, Chinese Baker has been picking out Egg Foo Young and Him Soon Pork from Column A and Fried Rice and Egg Roll from Column B since any of us can remember. See, that's *all* he eats. Hell, that's why they call him "Chinese." Anyhow, right then was when I knew there was another story, a bigger story, out there. But the problem was I had about four thousand words on this Chicago end-of-the-world cult who were planning a midnight leap from the Sears-Roebuck Tower between August 8th and August 15th (they wouldn't release the exact date), and an in-depth story about an albino family living in the sewer system of Milwaukee. I'd rigged the sewer family on my own, so I could come and go on that one, but the midnight leapers were true crazies, the real thing, and I had to stick around for that. Well, August 8th through the 15th comes and goes, and they announce that the mass leap was off until next year.

They had the right day and the right month, but they'd figured the stars wrong and come up with the wrong year. In the meantime, I'd missed Chinese's funeral.

On August 16th, I flew into LaGuardia and took a cab out Jerome Avenue to Woodlawn. It was there, all right. Up against a wall in Coach's Corner: a nice blue granite regulation football with Coach Buddy "Chinese" Baker carved on the seam. Under the stitching it read, "He Played for the Bear." After that they had his dates and the Oklahoma A&T records of two hundred and ten wins, sixty losses, twelve ties, Sugar Bowl '64, Cotton Bowl '66, '68, Orange Bowl '72, '76. And right across the bottom — "Roll On, Red Raiders."

Well, I made some notes about Coach's Corner and took about six closeups of the stone, and then another six with the George Washington Bridge and the World Trade Center in the background. As I was hanging around waiting for the shots to dry and finishing up my notes, a guy comes up and starts asking me questions. At first they sounded pretty dumb. How do I get paid? Do people rework my stuff? How many guys are over me? Things like that. But then I see he's leading up to something. Then it comes — he says for five hundred dollars he can put me next to the hottest story in the country. I waved him off on the five hundred, but when he said he couldn't go any lower because of the danger, I started listening. All of a sudden

I'm sold and I'm pealing off five big ones. See, we're on open-end expenses, so it's not costing me a dime, so I figure, why not? This guy, I'm going to call him Mike because he has a family, hangs out around this little deli over on Jerome, so he invites me over and after a couple of Budweisers, he's singing like a bird. He said the grave was a regulation eight by four by six, but that was the only thing regulation about it. Well, he says the kids around the neighborhood will spray paint anything, so he and his buddies sort of watch over Coach's Corner. Anyhow, the funeral was set for five last Wednesday and they were all dressed for the services. The word was out that Frank Gifford, Sam Huff, and Kyle Rote were coming out. But right at noon this hearse pulls up and right in here, Mike says, he starts getting suspicious, because the pallbearers didn't really look like pallbearers. It looked like they'd been drinking pretty heavy and they were walking too fast. He said they carried the casket out to the grave and then they looked around to make sure no one was looking, and they just shoved it in.

I said, "Shoved it in?"

"You heard me, mister. Shoved the damn thing in. No sermon. No services. Nothing. Hell, they didn't even use the lowering winch. They just shoved the thing in. I told my buddy Joe, see he works over there, that I guaranteed that thing had to split wide open." He popped open another beer and took a long, hard pull. Then he took a long, hard look at me. "Mister, if you're looking for a story, I guarantee it's right out there in Coach's Corner."

Well, the long and short of it was about two hours later his buddy Joe, who works the backhoe out here, has the grave opened and the dirt scraped back. Mike drops down in there with a crowbar and pries open the lid. Then he starts laughing. "Hey! This is crazy! It's full of books — *Reader's Digest Best Sellers.*"

After I shot a series of black and whites, Mike starts

handing them up. "Here's *Hawaii* — I always wanted to read that one. Joe, you want some? Here's *Jaws, The Agony and The Ecstacy, Love Story.*

"Sure, sure, anything. The kids will love them."

"How about you, McCoy? Name it."

"Yeah, give me that *Godfather.*"

"Here you go, pal. One terrific book. The movie didn't even touch it."

After we divided up about thirty books, we closed the casket, covered the grave, and headed back to the deli for a beer. Now, I could have gotten me a lawyer and a coroner and done a "Coach Chinese Baker Missing from Grave" story, and it would have been front page, right up there with "California Coed Drinks Blood from Skull of Murdered Lover," but, like I said, I go in for the in-depth stuff. See, there's always a chance for an anthology pick-up, and you've got foreign rights, and then there's Hollywood. I mean, they made a movie out of that Amityville crap, which didn't even run five hundred words. What I did was head into a bar near Madison Square where the old coaches hang out. After laying out three hundred dollars and then two hundred and then another two hundred, I find out that the morning line was still officially listing Chinese as dead for the public, but that he was actually alive and well near Tallahassee in a minimum security prison. I checked in with my boss, Vito DeAngelo, who's an old jock, and he says, "McCoy, I don't care what you're doing, drop it. I want that story."

Let me say something right here about DeAngelo. Not only does he own *The Midnight Enquirer,* he is also the best simulation photographer in the business. He wanted to come along, but he had an appointment at the Transcendental Meditation Center in Iowa. They'd been reporting levitations since 1976, but now they were claiming they could actually fly for short distances, and they wanted him there for the first shots. Well, I caught a plane to Atlanta, and then another to Tallahassee, rented a Hertz, and headed out.

This is the first time I've ever been this far south. Oh, I've been to Miami and Houston, but I mean this panhandle down in here is your basic South. The original swamp. "Impeach Earl Warren" is still out here on the smooth rocks and run-off culverts, and there's a lot of "Jesus Does Everything" copy running down the phone poles, and every road sign that's standing looks like Swiss cheese from being used for target practice. DeAngelo went to school down here in one of these pastures, and he says it's great. But I'll tell you one thing, I'd hate like hell being out here alone at night. Anyhow, I'm tooling along and trying to figure out how I'm going to interview Chinese Baker, because one of those two-hundred-dollar coaches had told me he had heard how Chinese wanted something. See, no one had actually seen or actually heard anything firsthand. Everything was somebody else seeing it, or somebody else saying it. Anyhow, he'd heard that Chinese wanted something. I figured it was money. But then, it could be drugs or women. Hell, maybe he just wanted a dog or a cat or a pair of gerbils. You never can tell about guys like that.

I hadn't seen Chinese since the Mud Wrestling Finals in Omaha and, well, I figured he'd be different. Well, let me tell you something — he *was* different. Instead of the old crew cut, drop seat, and Hush Puppies, Chinese Baker looked like he had just stepped out of *Gentleman's Quarterly*. He had on Calvin Klein everything: loafers, socks, beltless slacks with green and red insert panels at the cuffs, about a pound of gold chains around his neck, and a blue silk shirt that must have crossed the finish line at four hundred dollars. He was also tan. I mean dark, expensive, Virgin Islands tan, and he had his hair in a new, long, over-the-collar Barry Manilow look. The only problem was he had shot up from a low-slung one hundred and ninety pounds to a new low-slung two hundred and eighty. I didn't know Calvin Klein made clothes that big. One look around the room and I saw where it was coming from. He had his own bar, his own refrigerator, and his sideboard was loaded down with dessert cheeses and fancy English crackers and about a cubic foot of whole cashew nuts. He was also into imported beer: Lowenbrau, Heinekin's, Bech's, and about four other Japanese labels.

As I was plugging in my reel-to-reel, I saw his golf clubs and shoes stacked in the corner.

Flagler Minimum Security Prison. August 7th. Tape of Chinese Baker and *Midnight Enquirer*.

Enquirer: "Well, Chinese, how's the game going?" (It's always best to start an interview off away from the subject. You want the guy to relax and not let him think you're jumping down his throat.)

Baker: "Not bad. Let me show you something. The pro here says I've got a natural fade." (At this point, Chinese takes a five iron and shows me his new grip, his new stance, his new take away, and new finish. At Flagler Minimum, they have a golf pro, a tennis pro, a swimming pro, and a bowling pro. There are also two eighteen-hole championship courses, eight all-weather tennis courts, and over in the Charles Colson Health Spa Wing, enough Jacuzzi's and steam rooms and weightlifting machinery to service the Dallas Cowboys.)

Enquirer: "Well, that's great. O.K., now, Chinese. I want you to tell us in your own words exactly why you are here at Flagler Minimum Security."

Baker: "Because the NCAA ordered me here. They practically kidnapped me."

Enquirer: "They can't do that."

Baker. "What do you mean they can't? Look at me — I'm

here. They had a goddamn funeral for me. They want people thinking I'm dead."

Enquirer: "O.K. Why don't you just start from the beginning and tell us all about it."

Right in here Chinese punches the stop button. "Kid, I don't work for nothing. You catch my drift?" It boiled down fast — he wanted one hundred thousand dollars for the story. Well, I didn't waste any time either, so I called DeAngelo at the T.M. Center and he said, "Go for it." Three minutes later, Chinese and I are back with the tape rolling.

Baker: "After the Notre Dame game, the verdict came down that I was a disgrace to the high moral standards practiced by members of the NCAA Brotherhood of Coaches. That's the way they said it."

Enquirer: "They put you on trial or something?"

Baker: "Worse. They wanted me to go on with Cosell during the halftime on Monday night. They wanted me to apologize. Well, rat's ass, I couldn't do that. I mean, I had buddies out there and A&T alumni and all the old boys I played with. So I got mad and I told them to ram it. Well, I got in this thin-lapel lawyer out of Miami and we began going over the facts. He said the high moral standards line they were taking was our ticket to one of the biggest lawsuits in the country. Let me back up, McCoy. You see, I'm on staff for Recruiting Hotline. I was one of the damn pioneers, and the NCAA wants it kept quiet. So you see, we were in a Mexican standoff."

Enquirer: "You lost me, Chinese. I've never heard of any 'Recruiting Hotline.' "

Baker: "Well, if we're going to do this thing right, I'd better show you the setup. See, we try to keep a low profile."

He led me through into the back room, where he had a big IBM programming deck with a printout, and closed the drapes to cut the light bouncing in from the pool. The system worked like a Car Parts Hotline, only it was players and coaches instead of engine blocks and quarter panels. Chinese turned the unit on. "O.K., give me a college. Any college."

I rattled off, "Harvard, Yale, Princeton, University of Chicago."

He frowned. "No, I don't mean places like *that*. I mean *real* colleges. Places with *ball teams*."

"Arkansas, Penn State, Nebraska."

"Now you're talking. Watch. . . ." He asked the computer if Arkansas was looking for any talent. The answer came back: "Positive. Need white, combination football coach and minister. Forty to fifty. Must be Freewill Baptist. Married and willing to live on campus. No drunks, drug users, homosexuals. Salary forty-five thousand dollars plus church concessions and radio rights. Right man can take home eighty to one hundred thousand.

Chinese said, "This is peanuts. Let me show you something really interesting." He punched in Montana Mining in Missoula. "They're top bidders on this hotshot quarterback we're trying to place." A string of stars, asterisks, bars, and circles crossed the screen and he began translating: "O.K., three stars means Recruiting Hotline gets a hundred thousand up front. Two asterisks says the kid's not going north for nothing. He gets ten thousand a year, tuition, room and board, clothes, and a new Thunderbird. The two bars and circles means presidential waivers on SAT scores, criminal records, citizenship, catastrophic illness, everything. Also, if the kid can tie his shoes, he graduates and gets an inside shot on the Detroit Lions. It's what we call a nice tight package. The top of the line. Here, let me show you his profile."

The green copy ran across the screen: "Travis Mitchell, two hundred forty pounds, six feet five inches. Forty yards full uniform 4.5 seconds. Bench press three-ninety, 4.5 rushing avg. Completed twenty-five or more passes in thirty-six games."

"See, the kid does everything."

I said, "He's another Namath."

"He's better; he's seasoned. Here's his bio. 'Travis Mitchell, Lamar (Texas) High School. Three years All-Texas quarterback. Three years Mississippi Forest Junior College, three years Canadian Professional League. Will graduate Lamar High School this year. Parents (no religion) will cooperate with highest bidder outside Texas, Louisiana, Arkansas.' See, he's famous out there, so we'll ship him north or east. Montana Mining's ideal and they're in a rebuilding program. We're shipping them in a whole backfield and an assistant coach."

I kept looking at the screen and adding up the numbers. "Chinese, this kid's no kid. How old is he?"

"Oh, twenty-six, twenty-seven. What we do is keep them in high school five and six years, then they go to a junior college, and then two or three years in Canada, and then back to the feeder."

"But Jesus, a twenty-six-year-old guy graduating with those little kids? They don't even shave. And the girls, they're still popping bubble gum."

He shook his head.

"McCoy, you take your average eighteen-year-old kid who's dressing out at two-fifty, two-sixty. Well, that kid's too soft to play the kind of ball Recruiting Hotline stands behind. So we hold them back in the feeder until they hit top growth and get some experience. Three years in junior college and three more up in Canada and it makes a big difference. And I'll tell you one damn thing — you don't see all this knee trouble and shoulder separation crap you hear about. McCoy, you give the folks a winning football team and keep the injuries down, and it's four motorcycles to the

airport and four coming back. You can do anything." He
opened two more beers, went to the door and called out,
"Eino!" Then he said, "Want you to see Jerry before
feeding time."

Eino came in wearing thick padded gloves and a thick,
quilted chest protector. At first I thought he was handling
attack dogs. "McCoy, this is Eino, Eino McGovern. He's
Jerry's roommate. They played together back at A&T."

I stuck my hand out carefully. Eino was so big, he had
come in the door sideways. "Pleased to meet you."

He said, "Likewise."

Out back, Jerry was sitting in a truck tire swing. He was
hairy, all right, and as orange as a chow dog. When he saw
us he began jumping up and down and making this wild
clacking noise. From a distance he looked like he would
weigh in at around one hundred and wouldn't run any
taller than say four feet. But up close it was a different story.
The first thing you notice about a chimp is how long he is
when he stretches out. The second thing is how most of it's
arms. When Chinese patted him and scratched his head,
Jerry began smiling and sucking his teeth. They really
seemed fond of each other. Chinese handed me a tape
measure and told Eino to stretch out his arm. I measured it
at thirty-eight inches. Then he made Jerry hold out his. I
couldn't believe it, but there it was, sixty-one inches. Five
feet one inch — almost twice as long as Eino's.

Chinese took a long pull on his beer. "See, that was the
problem. Those damn arms were ridiculous." He scratched
Jerry's head. "O.K., baby. Show McCoy here how you used
to run. *Used to run, Jerry!*"

The ape moved out about twenty yards and began
jogging around us in a circle. "See how he's hunched over
and his hands are dragging the ground. See that *low*
running; I mean, people are dumb, but they ain't stupid.
That's what we had to work on. I had to get him up. I mean,

no one was going to buy this guy running around like that. O.K., Jerry! Show him how we run now."

Jerry's hands came up to his chest and he began bobbing around us in a sort of Groucho Marx lope. "See, I got the hands up and the elbows in. I'm also stretching him up four or five inches. But that's all I could get out of him. That's all there was. That's why I had this tailor come up with the pants to make his legs look longer. It's the old zoot suit style."

Chinese waved Jerry in. "Nice going, baby." He gave him a handful of cashews and let him finish the beer.

I watched Jerry tubing his lips around the beer can. The whole beer can, down over the label. "But damn it, Chinese, look at him. Look at his eyes. Look at his mouth. I mean, he looks like an ape. If I had to play against something like this, I'd call in the head linesman."

Chinese frowned. "Don't let him hear you talking like that. Watch . . . just watch."

In a few minutes he had Jerry dressed out in his Oklahoma A&T uniform. His helmet was cut closer than standard and closed his face in tight. He had on an oversized mouthpiece and a special faceguard. Then when he snapped on his extra-large chin strap and his dark glasses, all you could see were his nostrils framed with wisps of red hair. I took a long, hard look at him. I mean, I was up close, say two feet, maybe three, and I'd lay my hand right on the Bible if I could tell you *what* was under all of that equipment. "Chinese, I'll just be damned if I'm not sold one hundred percent."

"What did I tell you? O.K., Jerry, take it off. And don't throw it down, hang it up."

After Jerry stripped down, Chinese said, "I want you to feel some strength." I let him position me in behind Jerry and run my arms up under his armpits. Then he locked my hands behind his neck in a half nelson. For some reason —

maybe the beer was getting to me — I knew I had to trust him. But under that hairy back, I could feel something bigger and harder than just muscle. There was something down there pulsing and coiling, something hydraulic and terrifying. Right then I knew I'd give anything to be up on the Sears Tower with those end-of-the-world crazies, or with my albinos down in the sewer.

Chinese shouted, "Open your eyes! You've got to see this."

I looked up and saw one of Jerry's arms. His right, five-foot-long, powerful, hairy, red arm, and it was stretching up. Then I saw it gracefully curving back, and then gracefully coming down. His long fingers were closing all the way around my neck. Then I felt myself being lifted straight up and being stripped through that half-nelson and levered up and out and hung out there like a prize fish being photographed for a pier prize. Chinese was grinning.

"Strong, isn't he?"

I cleared my throat. "Yes."

* * *

Flagler Minimum Security Prison Interview with Chinese Baker and *Midnight Enquirer*:

Enquirer: "O.K., Chinese, the way I see it, there's no way Jerry can be out there on offense. Would you say that that was correct?"

Baker: "Damn right. See, it doesn't matter if I had him running like Tony Dorsett. He's still an ape, and we couldn't have him loping down the field. So I'd work him and Eino down the sideline for defense. Then we'd ease them in inside the ten-yard line. The only time we screwed up was when he grabbed that girl."

Enquirer: "Tell us what kind of reaction you'd get from the quarterbacks when Jerry tackled them, or did whatever he did to them?"

<u>Baker</u>: (sound of beer can opening): "You'd see them peering in there close, real close. See, they were trying to figure out why he was so strong. And how he got in there so fast. I've seen them get up with tears in their eyes. I don't mean tears of pain; I mean tears of pure terror. And you should have seen him tearing open a pocket. He'd throw them around like rag dolls. Come on, McCoy, drink up; I'm getting ahead of you."

I kept the tape rolling and Chinese kept talking. I mean he told me stories that even the *Enquirer* wouldn't touch. About an All-American tackle who played fourteen years in the Big Eight and Big Ten under three different names. About the secret Southern junior high school auctions where the parents parade the kids around like prize hogs and contract them out to the highest high school bidder. How hypnosis is used to keep the injured playing, and the use of torture and family reprisals out in the Rocky Mountain and the PAC Eight. He even had information showing how Oral Roberts psychs up their running backs to a suicidal intensity with the "Kamikaze-Jesus Run."

At the end of the day, I had nine hours of tape and four yellow pads of notes, and there was still more coming. About how the ACC and the Metro Eight use hallucinogenic drugs for the wide receivers and the boys on punt and kickoff returns.

"McCoy, if you think football's in bad shape, basketball's the same." He then told me how Texas L&J had contracted five Watusi lion fighters. "Kid, every one of them was over seven-feet-six; they came out of Zimbawee. God, you should have seen them; they were beautiful. And you should have heard their names; each one sounded like three or four people. The problem was, they would only play in the skin of the lion they'd killed. Shorts and shirts were women's clothes. There was also some talk, you know, of a little cannibalism. Hotline finally had to rule that they weren't college material. But last week we got a ripple from Vegas. They're talking about letting them keep their skins and hang on to their spears and shields and billing them as 'The Watusi Lion Killers' for the pro tour. Can't you just see them standing there on one leg with that equipment, and maybe some tom-toms and a medicine man, and taking on the Harlem Globetrotters? I guarantee the right promoter could make a bundle there."

I kept the tape rolling and the yellow pads going, and every half hour I'd have to shake my head, because I knew that this was going to be the greatest story *ever* told.

Around noon the next day, up comes the limo from the airport and in walks DeAngelo. He'd cut his trip short with the T.M.s and was down to get some action shots. For four straight hours he photographed Jerry tackling Eino, Jerry flipping out eighty-yard bullet passes with about a five-inch wrist snap, and Jerry stripping me through that half nelson. I've never seen him so wired. When he wasn't shooting, he was on the phone with production and advertising. We were jacking up the newsstand price to a buck and setting up for a twenty million press run. The advertisers had been fed the rumor that we'd found Jerry and were doing a whole issue on him and Chinese, and they were lining up like we were giving away Super Bowl tickets. Even Amy Richards, "The Golden Girl," who since my story had had two walk-ons in "Love Boat," had a press conference.

And then Chinese showed DeAngelo the Recruiting Hotline setup and filled him in on Travis Mitchell. Right away, DeAngelo began frowning and looking around the room and acting weird. Something had come unglued, but I'll be damned if I could put my finger on it. Well, the next time Chinese went to the john, DeAngelo grabs me by the elbow. "I've never heard of Recruiting Hotline! This is dynamite. That Mitchell kid is the hottest ticket in the country."

"Right, and this is going to be the hottest story we ever ran. Mr.DeAngelo, twenty million isn't going to touch it. Let's go thirty."

DeAngelo was nodding but it was for something else. "McCoy, I want that boy playing for me." He kept whispering as he told me his old team had had a two win and nine loss season for three years in a row, and that he was on the "search and seize" committee. "McCoy, we'd kill for that quarterback. I mean kill." The john flushed and in walked Chinese, zipping his fly and heading for the beer.

DeAngelo moved in fast. In less than an hour, with the console on and Chinese on one phone to Texas and another to Recruiting Hotline headquarters in Phoenix, and DeAngelo on another to his committee, the package was set and the check was signed. DeAngelo matched everything that Montana Mining had put up, but he had sweetened the pot by adding a Master's degree, a beach cottage for the summer, and fifteen guaranteed Miller Lite Beer commercials on graduation.

DeAngelo was wild with excitement and was calling everyone: *Sports Illustrated, The New York Times, The Wall Street Journal, The Christian Science Monitor.* But as DeAngelo's spirits went up, mine went down. The Jerry, Hotline, and Travis Mitchell stories were dead, and the minute Chinese sobered up, there was going to be hell to pay. After a big Mandarin dinner served with French champagne and strolling violins out on the Charles Ehrlichman Pavilion, and after Chinese had shuffled off to bed, DeAngelo and I were stretched out on the chaises by the pool. He was humming something, but I couldn't place the tune. Finally I said, "Just what do I tell Chinese? I mean, I gave him our word."

He said it slowly, carefully: "*Your* word, McCoy."

He started humming again. It was "Georgia."

I waited until he finished the refrain. "O.K., my word.

But what do I say? What in the hell do I tell him?"

I could see his sharp profile backlighted by the bar lights. "Tell him you lied." Then he raised up on his elbow. "We'll give him twenty-five thousand for his troubles. How's that grab you?"

"O.K., but it's still going to be a bitch telling him. Hey, what if *Esquire* or *Parade* comes in and wants to do it? It's bound to leak out now."

"McCoy, you think the NCAA and the NFL and the Gridiron Clubs around the country are going to stand still while that broken old jock makes a couple bucks and exposes something this big? Something this important? And look at the kids out there. Kids like Travis Mitchell. A kid like that should go to the best school in the country, and a kid like that should get the best money."

He suggested I pay Chinese off and leave in the morning for St. Louis. A story was breaking about how the Mafia was using the street Moonies for drug sales, and Reverend Moon was bitching about the accounting procedures. "I'm going to pull out of here tonight. Tell him it was an emergency."

"O.K., I'll do that. Hey, what happened at the T.M. Center?"

He groaned and stretched back out. "I'm getting fed up with those people. They sat around in that damn lotus position with their hands folded, and about every fifteen minutes one of them would make a little jump. More like a bump than a jump, if you ask me. Hell, I can get up higher than that. They wanted me to work up a shot of three or four of them flying around the building. You know, paint in some clouds and trees. I said screw it." He was quiet and lay there smoking. "You know, one of these days, I'm not saying tomorrow or the next day, but one of these days, I'd like to see the *Enquirer* get away from crap like that."

"Yeah, that would be nice." I was giving him about ten

percent of my attention. The rest was on planning how I
could quit the damn *Enquirer* and take the story to *The New
Yorker* or *Time* or *Newsweek.*

DeAngelo rolled on. "Ed, the way I see it, the country is
already on the ropes with crime in the streets and spiritual
isolation and nuclear tension. Now I'll admit we *have*
published some pretty flaky articles."

Inside I was whispering, "Flaky's the word. 'The Rise of
Homosexuality in the College of Cardinals,' 'Colorado
Coeds Rape Hare Krishna Leader.' " Then I ran through
Reader's Digest, Harper's, Atlantic. None of them sounded
right. None of them paid enough.

DeAngelo was in high gear. "Ed, but to tell the guys out
there that wax their Fords on Saturday and watch "Kojak"
and belong to the American Legion, in the middle of this
recession, that the NCAA is fattening and seasoning these
kids like they're beef cattle heading for the stockyards is just
too damn much. Kid, I'm saying this is different."

I nodded. Behind my teeth I was saying, "If that
quarterback wasn't around, it would sure as hell be
different; you'd be running it in red ink with purple
trim. . . ." Then I thought about *Rolling Stone.* They had
the money and the circulation and a pretty good art staff.
I'd probably have to slant the story for the rock-and-rollers
and the cocaine set, but that would be a snap. The real
problem was not to make the move until everything was
absolutely set.

DeAngelo kept rolling on. "Ed, you know what really
brings me down? John Wayne. Every time I see him, I have
to take off four inches for his lifts and three more for his
boots, because some son of a bitch decided that that was
news and the people should know about it. Ed, I'm saying
there are some things out there that people *do not* have to
know." He squeezed my elbow. "What I'm saying, old boy, is
we bury this one. Follow up on the Mafia-Moonie business,

finish your albino story, and there's a couple letters about Elvis being alive in Brazil. Maybe we can get a few sidebars out of it. How's that grab you?"

"Fine, Mr. DeAngelo."

"Call me Vito." His cigarette flared. "O.K., Ed. I know this is tough on you. Tell you what we'll do: When you come back, I'm putting you in a corner office and I'm putting you in there with a big fat raise."

"Thanks, Vito."

"And I want you to do some traveling and get this out of your system. There's a class action suit out in L.A. against a Cork and Closure Company. Claims they set up the Tylenol killings to sell safety caps. It's yours if you want it."

"Run that by me again."

"A screw top cap costs two cents; these safety seal jobs are around twelve. Kid, you multiply that out by twenty million and you're talking Pentagon dollars. It should be a dynamite story."

"No, that's too grim. I don't think so."

He sat still in the shadows. Finally he spoke. "O.K., Ed, what do you want to do? Take a vacation? Come home? You name it, because we owe you one this time."

"O.K., Vito, I'll tell you what. I want to stay here a couple days and let old Chinese down easy. You see. . . ."

"You don't have to explain." He tapped my shoulder. "Stay as long as you want."

The couple of days with Chinese turned into three days, four days. He told me everything there was about training Jerry and playing and feeding him, and everything there was to know about the Recruiting Hotline. I was matching him beer for beer and putting on weight like a Sumi wrestler. At night I'd lie there watching TV, and my stomach, and jiggling along with the Magic Fingers (The Salesman's Friend) and planning and re-planning my moves. I'd get a New York agent and we'd copyright the material and then go into the *Stone* headquarters and draw up the contract. Then we'd cross the road to Doubleday and make a book deal. Then I'd call DeAngelo and tell him to go to hell. I had it all worked out and it was perfect.

And then the next night I caught the Late, Late out of Miami. It was an old, low-rent, black-and-white called *The Knute Rockne Story,* starring, would you believe it, Ronald Reagan. I must have been pretty drunk, because instead of waiting till morning, I picked up four beers and went down the hall and woke Chinese up. "Chinese, what you've done with Jerry is a miracle."

He sat there in his shorts with his Heineken and cocked it on an angle. He smacked his lips. "Nothing like that first one in the morning." It was 4:00 A.M.

I gave him the miracle line again slower, and he said, "Yeah, that's what I've been saying all along."

"Chinese, we've got to get this story out to the American public."

He squinted up at me. "What's wrong with you, fellow? That's what we've been doing for a week now."

"I know, but just listen. Chinese, the way I figure it, you're too big for a magazine series. And you're too big for a book."

"Am I?"

"Chinese, I'm talking about a movie. Something big. Something bigger than big. Something like, say, *The Knute Rockne Story* or *The Alexander Graham Bell Story,* or hell, I'm talking about something like *Gandhi*. I'm talking about taking a couple years, and about a twenty million dollar budget, and openings all over the world, and with enough residuals coming in that you won't have to turn another hand from here on out. Can't you see it? *The Chinese Baker Story.* Simple and straightforward, just like that."

He brightened. "Yeah, now that would be nice. *The Chinese Baker Story*." But then I saw a shadow pass in behind his eyes. "You'd probably have to get somebody younger to play me in the early days, wouldn't you?"

I aimed my beer at him. "Paul Newman or Robert Redford would kill for a part like this. We'll have to beat them off with baseball bats."

His dark brows came together. "Too bad Duke Wayne's not around. But I got no problem with Newman or Redford. Butch Cassidy and the Sundance Kid. They're O.K. guys."

He seemed to be slowing down as he opened his second beer. "Ed, you know something? I wish you could have been there and seen Jerry against Wyoming. Yeah, and against Colorado." His eyes were warm and he was almost whispering. "And Notre Dame, now that was *the game*. Man, would I love to play that bunch again." There was a catch and a softness, almost a tenderness, in his voice when he said it again. "Yeah, Ed, I really wish you could have been there."

And then I saw the old boy in a completely different light. At first I thought it was the 4:00 A.M. beers. Then I saw it was something else; he really loved the crazy game. "Chinese, let me ask you something. If you had one wish, I mean one wish, right now, what would that be?"

"I'd be back on the bench coaching Jerry."

"More than the movie and the book and the articles? More than all the loot you're going to be making?"

"More than anything else. Ed, old buddy, I'm a coach. I ain't much of anything else, but I'm a damn good coach, and I want to be back out there coaching."

Maybe those pre-dawn beers didn't do anything for Chinese Baker, but they sure as hell did something for me. Because right in there I rewound and replayed DeAngelo's speech out by the pool. And as I did I remembered his byline over "Male Suicides Leap Thirty-Two Percent; Divorces Fifty-Four Percent During NFL Football Strike."

Then I realized what he was trying to tell me. If you destroy football, what do you replace it with? His idea of never ending *The Chinese Baker Story* was actually giving something back to the country, not taking it away. And right there, with old Chinese opening the beers and breaking out the chips and the cheese and the sun tipping up over the playing fields of Flagler Minimum Security, I got the idea and I called DeAngelo.

Well, the rest is history. It's not official history and it's not NCAA or NFL history, and it will never make the Guiness Book of World Records, but it's history nonetheless. One week later, one Fred Z. Murphy signed on with the University of South Georgia as third assistant defensive coach. At the same time, enrolling in the freshman class, with an SAT score of fourteen-twenty and four full years of eligibility, was one Jeffrey Kincaid out of Eugene, Oregon. Jeffrey lives off campus in a double-wide mobile home provided by the Board of Trustees with another Dean's List freshman from Eugene, Oregon, Ernest Dupree, a three-hundred-pound defensive guard. Both are majoring in communication, and since their courses are on closed circuit television, they are seldom seen in class and seldom seen on campus.

It's November now, and the winner of the Penn State-Pittsburgh game will be heading for Miami and the Orange Bowl to meet Alabama's Crimson Tide. The Big Ten and the PAC-Eight have three-way ties going into the last week, and the Georgia Bulldogs are still wearing black armbands since Herschel Walker began commuting from Sutton Place to the New Jersey Meadowlands. Down on the Atlantic Coast and across the South, the big news is still the number one team in the country, the gold-and-black South Georgia Golden Armadillos, who have literally crushed ten teams in a row and have yet to be scored on. The new chairman of the University of South Georgia Board of

Trustees, Mr. Vito DeAngelo, last week announced that
they have just accepted an invitation to play against Notre
Dame in the Sugar Bowl in New Orleans. Meanwhile, sports
writers over the nation are agreeing with the Las Vegas line
and are picking the Fighting Armadillos to win by at least
twenty-one points. They are also predicting that while the
Armadillos' Travis Mitchell probably will be the first
four-time winner of the Heisman Award, the big star down
here in the Piedmont is Jeffrey Kincaid, the camera-shy,
sensational, freshman nose guard, who is averaging more
than fifteen unassisted sacks per game within the ten-yard
line.

One Hundred Proof, Two Dollars a Gallon

W HEN I WAS a boy in Columbia in the early forties, Weaver Jeffcoat, who operated a bootleg shot house, hired me for a quarter an hour to sit on his porch swing as a lookout. Weaver sold a two-ounce drink for twenty cents, a half-pint for fifty, a pint for a dollar, and a half gallon for three. My job was to watch for the Law.

They came every week. Always out of the sun. Always in low, black Fords. Always fast. They'd charge hard, brake hard, and come sliding the last twenty or thirty feet with all four doors open. The sheriff and his deputies would hit the ground running, and in the boiling red dust of Calhoun Street, every neighbor on the block would gather in the drain ditch and every coon hound and yapper in the "Bottom" would join in the chorus. Weaver, who was a master plumber, carpenter, mason, electrician, and welder, and who could have made a good career out of any of the trades but chose instead to run moonshine back in the swamp and bootleg in town, had the porch wired. When I spotted the Law, I'd press a button, and Weaver would pull the plug on the whiskey he was storing in his fifty-gallon industrial sink. A straight four-inch pipe that looked more like an artillery piece than anything in the plumbing manual dropped the fifty gallons to the sewer in seconds, and by the time the Law had crossed the yard, rushed up the steps, flashed the search warrant, and made it to the deep sink, Weaver would be sloshing in coffee grounds or Clorox to kill the smell. The Law couldn't arrest for smell.

Weaver, a tall half-Cherokee who made good whiskey back in the Wateree Swamp out of half meal and half sugar in all-copper pot stills with lapped seams on the outside and no lead solder touching, had his own waffle-ridged bottles. He claimed a man could drink his whiskey in the rain and have no fear of dropping it. He used his own label: a black crow sitting on a barbed-wire fence, staring out into the middle distance over the caption *"100 percent pure corn, this is good whiskey."* At one point he even used his name on the label, figuring the woods were full of Jeffcoats and no one would know which one he was. But everyone did, and everyone trusted him to make good whiskey and hold the price down. With the U.S. government taxing the legal distilleries ten dollars a gallon and the state sliding in for more and pushing the over-the-counter price to roughly twenty-five dollars a gallon, it was simple mathematics: A man could buy almost four and a half gallons from Weaver for the price he would pay for one gallon of the tax-stamped bourbon from Louisville or Frankfort, Kentucky.

Weaver's career peaked and dipped several times from the thirties through the forties and fifties. At his crests he was a high roller, living up to his nickname, dressing in two hundred dollar single-button pinstripes and promenading down Main Street with women who looked like Mardi Gras floats. In the troughs he watched the Congaree River from the state prison down the hill in Columbia, or out across the fields from the federal prison in Atlanta. Every time he was caught for possession, whether it was in the swamp making, on the road driving, or in town selling, it was a year and a day. At one low point he gave me some good advice: "Never hit your brakes on wet blacktop, and, if you're going to commit a crime, make it federal — state time, little buddy, will break your health."

Years later, pressure and low money pushed him out of the business, and he moved on to Winnsboro. Since his driver's license had been revoked and every cop in town knew him, I became his driver when he came back to town. He still had his '39 Ford, but now the springs and shocks were shot and it wouldn't stay in gear. I drove. He drank. We'd wind down through the Bottom of Columbia, a scooped-out clay area that began behind the governor's mansion and ended a mile away at the state pentitentiary, and visit the old bootleggers running shot houses and all-night poker games. Most of the houses were in the no-phone, kerosene-lit section near the pen, and we'd sit around the oilcloth-covered kitchen tables, me drinking Pepsi Cola and feeding the trash burner in winter, or fanning myself with a funeral parlor fan in the summer, and listening to them talk and argue about the old days. There were five of them then — Smoke, Claude, Murdock, Amos, and Weaver — and they'd sit and drink and shout and lie. Sometimes they'd bet on some distant fact, and, after the money was counted and stacked, I'd go out to a phone and call the newspaper to check out what year Rufus Babcock shot Sally Motes, or who married Cora Rideout, or how much capacity the big Camden still of '39 had and who was the sheriff who cut it down. For some of the questions, the paper had no answers.

I remembered Smoke, a smoke screen artist who talked a mile a minute. "Weaver . . . Weaver . . . dammit, Jim Buck

Reynolds invented the Jumbo Still. You remember him.
Drove a B-model Ford. Long old boy, had something
wrong with his knee. Hell, you get down in near Kingstree
and that thing's *called* the Jim Reynolds." Weaver was eating
boiled peanuts. He always ate boiled peanuts when he
drank.

"No way, Smoke. My uncle brought it over from
Valdosta. I was there when he drew the damn plans. You're
thinking about the 'ground hog.' "

"I'm telling you it was the Jim Reynolds. It was. I tell you
it was."

"Reynolds stayed drunk nine days out of ten. He wasn't
no distiller."

Smoke didn't let up. "Weav, there's two hundred
Reynolds down in them woods. You just got the wrong one.
Remember how he couldn't get out of a car unless he slung
his leg over?" Gus Caso shot him up on Laurel Hill."

Weaver had the last word. "I got the right Reynolds and
the right still. Only thing that came out of Kingstree was
third stage malaria and the 'ground hog.' The Jumbo came
out of Valdosta."

Both Weaver and Smoke were in on the big steam still set
up across the Georgia line in 1932. The story ran they
bought a sheriff off for three months and installed the first
three-shift steam operation in South Carolina/Georgia
history. The average still needs only four or five days to
show a profit, but, with three months to work and the sky
the limit on size, Weaver, Smoke, and the boys from
Georgia went for broke.

Weaver pulled the soft shell from a purple nut meat.
"Hell, we had super-heaters up twenty-two feet, and
thirty-six eight-hundred gallon mash vats. Now you talk
about some timber — we had it, Horse. We damn well had
it."

Smoke rolled in. "Delco plant for juice, electric pumps

for mash feeders and water, thirty or forty lights, gasoline-fed Detroit burners. Hell, that thing turned on like an airplane engine. You could see the leaves rustling a hundred yards away."

Claude asked, "How much was that sheriff taking?" Smoke said, "Plenty. And when he saw how big we were getting, he came in for more."

Weaver interrupted. "Man, we looked like E. I. DuPont out there in those Georgia woods. And talk about whiskey. We were reading sachrometers and had that yield up to eighteen out of a sack of sugar. Blending in at eleven hundred and twelve hundred a day. . . . Multiply it out. Eleven hundred gallons times ninety days. . . . Brother, we were making whiskey."

Claude, a practical man with a slide rule behind his eyes, closed them. "You're talking about one helluva lot of sugar."

"Brought a boatload up from Cuba. Right up the river to Columbia. Friend, we had a warehouse as long as a football field."

A breeze cut through the small room, and in the orange light of the kerosene lamp, their long shadows flapped on the pine walls. "I had me more cars and suits and shoes back then than I could count. Had a Chris-Craft motorboat tied up at Ballentine's Landing, two cooks and four drivers." Smoke smiled, "And a couple women, too." Weaver nodded. "A couple . . . but it's all gone now. Gone. Seems like it all just streaked by."

Smoke soft-punched Weaver's shoulder. "We had us some times though, didn't we, old buddy?"

"We had 'em, Smoke. We sure as hell had 'em."

It's been a long time since I've been over Weaver's old route through the Bottom. The hurricane-fenced penitentiary still looms against the river and the moon, and through the doorless shotgun houses you can see the Ford and Chevy shells in the weeds behind. That old mole, Time, has cocked the houses and slid them sideways on their brickbat corners and twisted them with the wind, and the sloping clay keeps washing down, down to the old red Congaree. Wisteria, azalea, and chinaberry have overgrown and spider-webbed the roofs, the chimneys, the car shells, and the fences, and when it blooms in March it's stunning. But in December, when the roots are bare and clutching and everything's the dusty color of a hornet's nest, the tiny porches without steps or spokes, and the doorways without doors, the empty, echoing rooms are fragile and strangely vulnerable.

Weaver is dead and buried in North Georgia, and Smoke and Claude and Murdock are all long gone. The only one left is Amos, who lives alone with two dogs and a domesticated squirrel named Horace. Amos in his heyday had leopard skin upholstery and Mexican ball fringe around the windows of his souped-up '37 Ford, and was one of the best "rods" on the road. Once, caught in a police trap on the one-way wooden Gervais Street Bridge, he backed off at full throttle, fishtailed over the two-lane blacktop until he sucked the Law into a drain ditch, and then powered out and away. He was hot. One night, coming in from Augusta with seventeen cases leveled out below the windows, he pulled into a honkey-tonk for a beer. He had more than one, and then, covering a big bet on the counter, picked up the phone and told the sheriff he was running that night, heading due east on the Leesville Road. Amos spent five of his prime years in jail, had a Lee Roy Yarborough reputation for dirt road chases, and was a demon with the ladies. Now he splits his time between the Methodist Church and television. He didn't want to talk about the old days. "Billy, I swear I want to forget that mess. I got other things I'm studying."

I'd brought along two six-packs of Miller's, and finally, after we'd sat through a "Dragnet" rerun, he reached for one. As he drank, a new light replaced the hard caution in his eyes, and his thin face seemed to flesh out. "You ought to go out and see old Slick. Now there's the boy that can tell you something." Horace, the squirrel, eased down the chair arm, and Amos poured him some beer in the ashtray.

"Sligh?"

Strother "Slick" Sligh had been the sheriff they'd butted heads with, and the only driver who could match them mile for mile on the Augusta-to-Columbia road and down through Hell Hole Swamp.

"Right. I did five years and five days because of that scutter, but I'm telling you he was straight. Straight as they come. I was there when they offered him ten thousand dollars to leave the Gervais Street Bridge open for one night so we could haul stuff in. Ten thousand dollars. Now that was money then. Turned us down flat. Lot of those monkeys were getting fat taking ten percent from the still man, ten from the shot houses, and ten more from the wholesaler. Hell, they had more things going than you got fingers and toes. But not Sligh. That old boy's motto was 'If you can't do the time, don't commit the crime!' . . . You know why they hired him?" He cut the sound off on "The Dick Van Dyke Show" but left the picture on. "Speed. That's why they call him 'Slick.' 'Slick' Sligh. He was as fast as a deer. Hell, he'd run you down in the woods and tie you to a tree and then run on and catch your buddy. Then, when he got too old to sprint, he trained him a dog. Talk about something embarrassing, how'd you like to have a damn coon hound tree you? But I tell you the God's own truth, out of all that whole pack back in there, he was the only man I respected. If you go see him, you tell him I said hello."

"Tell me something about stills."

"Well, we had some pots, some steams. Hey, that's a pretty big subject."

"Say you were giving a lecture about them."

He scratched Horace's small head and rubbed his tiny ears. "Well, you'd have to begin with the mash. We'd run anything — sugar, meal, maybe throw in a little bran. Sugar was higher than meal back then, and it worked faster, but there was always plenty cornmeal around. You get your better whiskey out of straight corn."

He popped another beer. "First off you get your mash boxes. We'd use nine or twelve or fifteen, on up to thirty-six. As long as you could divide it by three. That way one third's cooking, one third's making, and one third's getting ready. Minute you load one batch into your cooker, you mix another batch in the empties. That way you always got something getting ready to run. Once you get started, you don't want to stop. Got me?"

"Right."

"Boxes were all the same. Four by four by four. Made them out of one-by-fours. Then take another slat and batten up the sides. We'd use the greenest pine we could get. That way they'd swell up fast and get tight. We'd pick up a little turpentine on that first run, and we'd sell that a little cheaper. But then, on our second run, we'd come in right on the old nail head. When I first got into it, we'd start up at first light with pine knots and then switch over to hickory so it wouldn't smoke. Later on we converted to gas, you know, propane. Hell, we even used straight gasoline. Everything depended on where you were and what kind of rig you were working. We used a lot of coke, too. That doesn't smoke at all."

He explained how they would build a still a day for four days and then start bringing in the men and the supplies. "If the sheriff wasn't hitting, we'd lay back on the building, but, if he was cutting and dynamiting, we'd send a sapper in after him and salvage burners or cooker caps and keep on building. That cap was the thing that took the work. All hand-hammered, we used to flare them out like a tuba bell, and I mean they had to fit right or you had trouble. . . . Old Zuck had him about five rigs going one time. Fast as he'd set up and get going, the Law would cut him down. Round and round. He was going crazy. Must have built fifteen units, and I bet he didn't make dime one. . . . Most of the time you can get by with one or two; that way you can watch your quality. We weren't selling no junk back then. It was all second-run copper kettle and beating anything they were shipping out of Louisville." Horace finished the beer and wanted some more, but Amos cut him off. He popped another for himself. "Of course, back in then we had the time, and we could throw a little age on our stuff. Makes a big difference. Six months is all you need, and it mellows down nice and gives you a nice echo taste. . . . You going to print this?"

"Yes."

"Well, let me tell you something. These monkeys running around now saying they know this about whiskey and they know that about whiskey couldn't find their ass with both hands. You print this. You take a cheap bottle of vodka and a cheap bottle of scotch and mix them in a Chivas Regal bottle, and you won't get one complaint out of fifty. That's the kind of information the public ought to be knowing. Hell, they can fight this recession with some facts like that. The only way to know anything about whiskey is to make it. You read those ads about aged natural spirits and that garbage about gin and vodka. All lies. You can't age something that's neutral, and they shouldn't be advertising like that. How in the hell can the public check that out? You know what we used to figure a gallon of whiskey cost to make? I mean making it, jarring it, and getting it to town? Thirty-six cents, and that's all of it. All it is is meal and sugar and water. Mostly water. Tell me something: How's some poor old West Virginia ridge runner going to afford thirty bucks a gallon when he ain't making thirty a week? He can't, so the wives get kicked, and the kids go hungry. I'm telling you, there's two sides to this story, and people only heard one. The liquor lobbies, that's where it all comes from. The government doesn't care about a little corn whiskey. Hell, most of your revenue boys are ex-moonshiners anyhow; they know what's up. But the big distilleries get in there and lean on the government to get rid of the moonshiner. Then what happens? We get wiped out, and here comes your fast runners, Jack-rabbiters. In and out. In and out. Make a batch and move on. In and out. Don't care what they put up and don't care who gets hurt. Running it through car radiators and galvanized steel and God knows what they're throwing in there to speed up that mash. They're selling pure-out poison. No doubt about it, and folks shouldn't buy it. But I'm saying we ought to spread the blame a little smoother. I'm saying the government ought to step up to Mr. Walgreen's drug store and raid those rack of *rub* he's selling. Hell, those heads can get it for a quarter a quart. Now that's the stuff that's mean. One hundred percent wood alcohol, for external use only. It'll kill you quicker than a train."

We talked about stashes. Bottled whiskey had to be hidden, and hiding places ranged from tree-tops and attics and sliding panels to blackjack trees potted in ten-gallon cans covering an underground stash of three or four hundred gallons. Stumps, creek bottoms and simple holes worked in the country. Amos grinned. "I had me an old long dog that would find it for me. No lie. I'd plant ten or twelve jars out in the road. Old sandy road with ruts on each side. I'd lace it down the middle. Put it there so I could get it quick. Then when I went to get it, I'd forget where it was, and pretty soon this old dog would nose it up. Hell, that fool could smell anything. Mixed breed. That's the best kind. You couldn't give me a damn pedigreed."

I asked him about the sundown law, an unwritten code which prevents the Law from raiding after the sun goes down. "Guess that started back in the olden days. You'd have to look it up. But, man, it was rough down in here, say, around 1910. They had some characters running around you wouldn't believe. You know we had the same gun laws you had out West. I mean, if someone was to draw on you and you got him first, that was that. He was paid for. One old boy, I forget his name now, dammit; I heard it the other day. Real hothead. Hell, he'd deliver whiskey with a buggy and a race horse. Now he had style. He got so brazen with it, he set a barrel of whiskey out on the street corner on a table and put a cup on it with a sign that said *For Police and Constables Only.* He didn't give a damn about anything. They hit him one night, and he hollered, 'Don't come in here. The sun's down, and my wife's dressing.' They came in, and he cut 'em in half with a twelve gauge. They tried him and all, but turned him loose. Right about in there they started laying off raiding after that sun dropped. I don't think it's a law. But I'd say it was a very strong practice."

A night game started on the television. Amos is a Chicago Cubs fan. He began telling me about different stills, including the legendary horse blanket model. "Funny, you never see them in westerns. But that was the only thing they used out there. Couldn't get near a stream to cool their condensers, so they had to set up right out there in the dust. Tell you what: If you're putting this in print, you tell them it's as simple as one, two, three. Matter of fact, it's the best way in the world to understand how to make whiskey." He popped open two beers. The squirrel's small tongue was darting in and out, and his black eyes were shining. "You take your regular mash, say, half sugar, half meal, and scald it down with boiling water. Then you let that slurry set for three days until it starts in to working. If it's hot weather, maybe a shade less than three; if cold, a little more. We used to top it with bran in cold weather to hold it in. . . . O.K., now then, once that stuff is fermenting, you put it over your fire and start cooking." He grinned, "I'd make a helluva TV personality, wouldn't I? You know, something like Julia Child or the Galloping Gourmet. . . . Anyhow, after that mash starts cooking, you slap your horse blanket over it. Then you set back and wait. . . . When that blanket starts sagging down with that steam, you take it off and run it through your clothes wringer. You got to understand that this is one sorry way to make whiskey. Probably wouldn't get one-tenth the production you would from a pot, but I guess that's all they had to work with back then."

"Must be pretty fierce tasting."

"Probably ten times better than this crap they're running around town now. At least there's no way of getting any lead poisoning. That's what's giving whiskey such a bad name around here."

I asked him about the stories of possums dropping into mash vats and dying there.

"That's all propaganda. Why, the possum is one of the smartest animals in the woods. I'd say the odds of a possum dropping and dying in a mash vat are about four million to one. Hell, he uses that tail of his like a fifth leg. He'd have to be climbing out on a limb and get a heart attack or a stroke to fall in. Boy, that animal is *nimble*. . . . Course, a revenue man could catch one and dip him in and then hold him up for a camera shot. It would make a fine picture."

He talked about setting up a still in a two-story house four blocks from the jail. "Oh, we were young and crazy as hell. We figured the closer we were to the jail house, the less we'd be suspected. But it worked. Worked fine. Ran that thing for five or six weeks. The top story was the still, and the bottom was rigged for storage and funnelling off the mash slop through the toilet. . . . Man, we had portable stills back in the forties. You know where I-26 crosses Broad River?"

"Sure."

"That used to be a cow pasture. We set one up right in the middle of it by a little old creek. Dug us a bunch of post holes and planted pine trees and blackjacks in buckets for a screen. Steam rig too, thirty-six mash vats, about four hundred gallons a day. Me and old Buck would work and watch. We were using coke, so there wasn't any smoke, and we'd sit out there and count the cars coming by and bet quarters on what kind was coming next. You know: Ford, Chevy, Plymouth, Buick. Funny, we worked that setup for about four weeks, and, just as we were pulling out, the trees were going brown and dropping their leaves. Now, how's that for timing?"

New York scored four runs, and he cut the picture off. "We had some clever operators back then. One boy had a still in a semi-truck. No lie, he'd pull up to a trailer court, plug in gas and electricity, and he was in business. Another one sunk him one down in a bomb shelter. That wasn't too long ago. Didn't work. Didn't vent it right, and he died during the first run. Told him to watch that venting, but that fool wouldn't listen. Now what was that old boy's name? Damn, I can't remember anything anymore. You got to watch that air when you get in that close. That gas will eat up your oxygen, and then you got troubles. But you take on the average, we were one helluva lot smarter than the revenue boys chasing us. Lot of times they'd jump the force and join up with us. We were making money hand over fist, and they were getting paid off in scrip. And I mean, if you weren't smart or couldn't drive or do something, there just wasn't any place for you. You had to be special and you had to be good at a lot of things. Of course, that Hollywood crowd has gone and ruined it by making us look like we were Snuffy Smith hillbillies. Hell, there were a lot of college-educated boys running around with us. You know what we did one time when the Law was clamping down on buying sugar? Went out and bought three freight cars of cinnamon rolls. No lie, and I mean they worked like a charm. Only problem was messing with all those wrappers. You know, right this minute, I can still feel the frosting. And talk about money, there just ain't no telling how many millions came through this doggone town. I bet half the politicians back in there were backed by whiskey money. Those bricks in the state buildings might be cotton money, but I'm giving long odds that most of that fancy woodwork and those chandeliers is Carolina corn."

I asked him if all his crowd were alive today and had the money and time, how they would set up.

"Let me see now, that's a pretty tall order. . . . We had the brains, all right. And nerves like cold rolled steel." He drank and poured out an ounce for Horace and stroked his black and tan hound. "Well, I'd get me a ship and lay off the coast. I'd run into Cuba and get me all the sugar I needed and all the grain. You could even stock up on soybeans. Now there's something I bet no one's ever tried. . . sure you can print this?"

"Positive."

He burred his ball-point into his ear and examined the wax. "Well, if I had me this ship and I was captain, I'd rig up a steam outfit with a vacuum pump and a refrigerated condenser, and I'd make it. I'd solid make it. I'd recycle that mash slop and sell it back to the Cubans for their hogs. Hogs love it. They get drunk and dreamy-eyed, but they lap it up. Tell you something else; it does wonders for the bacon. Your problem might be in getting it to market, but, once you were rolling, all that would fall into place. You take along the Carolina coast; there's four thousand miles of inlets down in there. It would be like a gambling ship, only it would be a helluva lot better odds. . . . Hey, what if some Hollywood producer sees this and wants to do a TV series?"

"He'd have to use you as the story consultant."

Amos laughed and ran Horace's gray-brown tail through his fingers. "Maybe Slick could help out. He'd tell one side; I'd tell the other." He popped open another beer. "Now that would be a show worth seeing. We'd probably have to change the names and all. . . . But man, we could solid tell the stories."

Iowa State Fair

PART OF LIVING in Iowa and celebrating surviving the winters is summer and the fairs. There are country fairs, town fairs, and fairs jimmied up at the crossroads, with sawhorse tables for the pies and the pickle relishes and rides that fold down from the backs of pickup trucks. There are the Solon Beef Days, the Great Jones County Fair, the Old Settlers and Threshers Reunion, and the world-famous Centerville National Pancake Day, where more than a quarter of a million free pancakes and coffee are served to anyone who can get there. But the big one out here is the Iowa State Fair. The Texas extravaganza has more and bigger of most everything, but the Iowan's pride is that when Hollywod shot the movie *State Fair*, they came here. For a dollar twenty-five, old posters are available of Pat Boone and Ann Margret singing their hearts out to "I Love Iowa" with the Des Moines capitol dome shining gold in the background.

One hot, humid summer day, I turned my air conditioner to supercool and, with a load of kids, rolled onto

Route 80 heading west to the fairgrounds. The two-hour drive had sharpened the kids' appetites, and after waving off the John Birchers dressed in American flag double-knits and hawking their strange titles near the admission gate, we headed for the chuck wagons. At the Freewill Baptist Tent, the ladies behind the ladles served us country-fried steak smothered in onions and gravy, mashed potatoes, cole slaw, hot biscuits, and cherry cheese pie. The kids ordered double milkshakes. In front of us on the promenade the Marine marching band was red, white, and blueing it into "Halls of Montezuma," trying to lure the few good men they wanted out of the corn and soybeans to exotic places at high pay. And sixty feet up in the sky, slim Danny Sailor, "The World's Champion Tree Climber and Tree Topper," was leaning back in his leather waving to his many friends and admirers. From the grandstand a roar went up, and higher than Danny was "Icarus, the Bird Man" with yellow rockets streaming from his kite wings while the announcer intoned, "One false move at that altitude, folks, and old Icarus is in deep trouble."

We headed for the clatter of the midway, and the noise, the music, the sawdust triggered some madness in me from the past. I had a grape slush in one hand and a caramel nut apple in the other. I was eating what the kids ate, seeing the shows they saw and riding the rides they rode — the double Ferris wheel, the Whip, the Octopus, the Mouse.

The two-headed-baby show was in a low-rent half stall with a dirt floor. Outside, the ticket taker, who looked like he was wanted for armed robbery, announced they had just joined forces with the medical profession in its heroic fight against birth defects and mental retardation. (Doctors and nurses with proper credentials were admitted free.)

We stopped for pizzas and Ice Cream Delights (a stick of ice cream dipped in chocolate and rolled in nuts), then to the roller coaster and the revolving barrel. And then the tall, thick, chain-driven tower at the end called simply "The Zipper." You stand up and hold on while it takes you slowly to the top for a gentle rock and a view of the fairgrounds. Then it slams into some incredible one-to-one-thousand gear ratio, and all hell breaks loose. Kids weep, women scream, and grown men groan. In one second I was standing on my head, in another I was corkscrewed, turned inside out, and shaken until my teeth rattled. It's legalized pickpocketing, and the whipping torque took my glasses, my change, my wallet. It's a terrible ride; probably illegal, certainly lethal. I came staggering out, grateful to be alive. The kids came falling down in the sawdust laughing and crying and dying to go back again.

Our next stop was the inflated vinyl jumping moon room. The air conditioning was out, and the hundred-and-ten-degree heat was rising. We came out gagging. Two of the kids lay in the shade of the House of Mirrors rubber-legged and glassy-eyed, looking like their next ride would be to the infirmary. The other three were ash-gray and docile. But in four minutes they were walking, in five they were hungry, in six they wanted to ride the bumper cars. The heavy Baptist food, the whipping, spinning, splaying of the Zipper, and the heat visions of the moon room had gotten to me, and the handwriting was clearly on the wall. I gave them money and mumbled something about meeting a friend someplace. When I turned to see if they were watching my retreat, they were streaking like whippets straight back to the Zipper.

The hot blacktop was melting, and my shoes made sucking sounds as I headed for the trees. Unlike most fairs which fan out from the midways like Mississippi floods in the springtime, the Iowa State Fair has a seventy-year-old, red-brick administration building in the center, with a porch running around all four sides. Oak trees shade it; thick grass cools it. There are benches for the weary, picnic tables for the families, and free entertainment for all. Continuous amateur shows go on and on and on; accordion solos to "Midnight in Paris," tap and acrobatic dancing to "Tico Tico," hands folded together for solemn renderings of "Yearning" and "Because," and heavyset baritones pleading for "Stout-Hearted Men." This may very well be the last outpost of innocence.

Inside the administration building, twelve children had been lost for the day, but they'd been sorted out and picked up. The record is thirty. I crossed over the cool grass under the shade oaks to Pioneer Hall. Mrs. Hazel Dean's bread-and-butter pickles, winner of blue ribbons at Madison, Union, and Adair County Fairs, hadn't traveled well to Des Moines, and the judges weren't impressed. But Mrs. Dean had more than just pickles. She won second in best quilting, fourth in patchwork quilting, third in hamburger buns, and back-to-back seconds in angel food and chiffon cakes.

At the Poultry Barn, champion Kathy Screiber of Lone Tree, Iowa, didn't let the bettors down. She coasted into first place with her old-fashioned delivery of "contented chicken clucking" and brought the house down with her "angry hen at egg plucking time." Other contests surged and rattled on: the seven-thousand and twelve-thousand pound Tractor Pull, the thunder-and-smoke-filled Demolition Derby, the World's Champion Exhibition of Montana Sheep Shearing, Cake Decorating, Horseshoe Pitching, Hog Calling, and the Annual Ladies' National Nail Driving Contest.

At the Cattle Barn it was naptime for the big black and white Holsteins after their marathon milking exhibition. I left and crossed the road into another barn, another culture, the Swine Barn.

Now I've always wanted to know a little something about hogs. I asked a short, serious judge in a yellow skimmer what they looked for in a championship hog. "Friend" —

this man had all the facts — "we judge hogs on one point
and one point only: how much meat that fellow can deliver.
If there's one extra pork chop on that hog, I don't care if
he's got one eye and four ears, that hog is number one." He
tapped me on the arm. "Raising hogs is a business, friend.
This ain't no kennel club." He kept calling me friend.
"Friend, you got to figure the less overall fat, the more hog
you'll get for your money. Now take a fat wide fellow with a
lot of extra jowl hanging down. That hog ain't good for
nothing. And I mean nothing, in my estimation, turns a
judge off faster than a hog that can't walk."

The hog judge stayed in high gear. "Pork chop buyers
don't care about breeding. What they want is a hog that's
hitting top growth in two years." He explained hog
classifications: up to fifty pounds is a pig, fifty to
seventy-five a shoat, over that's a hog. "Now take a big boar
like that fellow over there or a sow that's been around. Hell,
they'll top out at seven hundred to eight hundred pounds.
I've had to use forklift tractors to pull them out of drain
ditches in the wintertime. I ain't kidding."

He shifted into meat economics. A pound of beef
requires seven and a half pounds of feed corn; a pound of
pork four and a half pounds; poultry, two pounds. He went
on to how the best and the most hogs are raised in Iowa,
because of the feed corn. "Last year we shelled so much we
ran out of silos and had to stack it at the crossroads. Friend,
you talk about your number ones, Iowa raises over
one-fourth of all the corn and hogs in the whole country.
Wasn't for us, New York and California would be down on
their knees starving. I mean *starving*." He tubed his lips,
watching a long-legged coed in a University of Iowa "Go
Hawks" T-shirt jiggling by, checking her for extra cuts and
leaner bacon. "Hey! That gal ain't wearing no brassiere."

I asked him why, if everything was so slide-ruled out for
the butcher counter, the owners hot-combed and pow-
dered them before showing. "Well, friend, it's the exact

same reason a girl will primp in front of a mirror. Showmanship! They want that hog to step out there with the best possible chance." He handed me a tract and a bumper sticker, HOGS ARE BEAUTIFUL. "We're out to improve the image of the hog and maybe bring a little of that beef money down to us. Lots of people figure hogs are dirty and will eat anything you put in front of them. Friend, you give a hog a chance and he'll live a lot cleaner than most people. . . ." So much for hogs.

I returned to the kids. They had been sitting on their hands on the roller coaster, riding backwards on the double Ferris wheel, and doing quick handstands on the upstroke of the Zipper. They were broke; they were hungry. We ate barbecue, tacos, caramel corn, and more Ice Cream Delights. We pitched dimes, threw hoops, shot basketballs, tried to knock down the solid iron milk bottles, and drove the bumper cars. We rode some more, ate some more, saw the rest of the shows, and headed for the grandstand, where they flashed between the seats and the hot dog and cold drink stands like it was a relay race.

It was first dark and the show opened. Jerry Clower in his red silk master-of-ceremonies suit told how as a Yazoo City, Mississippi, farm boy he had found station WHO, Des Moines, on his radio and set the dial and tore off the knob. He did his famous "Coon Hunt" and "Maurice and the McCullough Chain Saw" stories and brought the house down. He then introduced The Haggers of "Hee Haw" fame. The big lights dimmed. The pin lights picked them up racing across the stage laughing wildly at something that must have happened backstage. Their red-hot, ice-cold material, old when Fibber McGee told it, hung in the air like fertilizer dust. It was a long act, and a woman behind us warned her brood, "Now, don't go clapping or they'll just *stay* out there."

The grandstand crowd are gun-shy about Nashville and Hollywood stars. They've been burned before by short shows, bad shows, no shows, and outright insults. Several years back Johnny Cash's M.C., who had been looking at too many interstates and too many secondary gravels, committed the cardinal sin when he proudly announced, "Big John is glad to be back among his own kind of people. Yessir, he's proud to be back in *Springfield, Illinois*."

Midnight and a last zip on the Zipper, milk shakes, and Pronto Pups and back to the parking lot. Out on the open road, the stars came down to the edge of the night, and the twinkling lights of the small crossroad towns were blue in the distance. Sixteen-geared semis rumbled by heading west to Denver and east to Chicago, with fifty thousand-watt, clear-channel WHO running down the barbed wire all the way to the panhandle. The kids were re-riding the rides, reliving the shows — "Naw, I didn't believe any of that. . . . Wonder how much that Zipper thing cost. I mean, like you wanted to buy it."

They began whispering and preparing a thank-you speech. The paper boy cleared his throat and rattled off that they would do yard work, dog work, anything I wanted. I screwed the cap down on my Jack Daniels and made him promise for the seventeenth time that on rainy mornings he would fold the *Des Moines Register* and put it in the mailbox. "You got my word, I swear it."

Another voice, slower. "Boy, you better."

They were suddenly quiet. Then . . . "You ask him." "No, you." A truck stop was shining in the distance. Getting them by it would be like asking a rabbit to deliver lettuce. I took somebody off the hook. "Anybody hungry?"

We pulled in between the big Mack rigs and the Diamond Reo's for cheeseburgers, French fries, apple pie, and Pepsi Colas. And later, listening to Merle Haggard on the juke and watching the catsup splatting on the fries and the flying forks and the diesels refueling out under the neon and the night, I decided if you're ever going to The Fair, this is the way to do it.

Grand Ole Opry

T HE NASHVILLE winter of 1974 was the Grand Old Opry's last season at the Ryman Auditorium, its home for thirty-three years. The one hundred and fifty singers, pickers, comics, and cloggers, who must agree to make twenty-one appearances each year to become members of the Opry company, had agreed to play down any misgivings they might have about moving out to the new Opryland, and four- and five-color brochures urged, "Come Share the Wonder of OPRY-LAND, U.S.A., where the best of country music blends with the strains of Bluegrass, Dixieland, Western, Rock, and all of the other exciting sounds of music from this great wide country of ours."

Roy Acuff, the veteran "King of Country Music" whose rendition of "The Wabash Cannonball" is a country anthem, reportedly said he was glad to be moving out the nine miles on Route 40 East, that old Ryman was a firetrap, that he was worried about the walls falling down. But there were cynics like the beer drinker I talked to at Tootsie's

Orchid Lounge, the tavern behind Ryman Hall that has acted as a watering hole for many of the stars and sidemen: "Why shouldn't old Roy want to move?" he asked. "Ain't they naming that roller coaster out there 'The Wabash Cannonball?' By God, this is one old boy that ain't setting foot inside that place. Hell, you can't even buy a beer out there." And a producer on Nineteenth Street, the center of the music publishing business: "Honey, I'm never going in there again. I went once and I had to leave. I began crying. Crying. That was the worst thing they could have done to country music. Oh, I just hate it. All that plastic and Astroturf. And that air conditioning is going to ruin country music. A country boy has got to sweat or he ain't nothing."

The final performance at Ryman Hall on March 9, 1974, in the old red-brick tabernacle, with the oak floors, the hand-carved pews, the ecclesiastical windows, the tiny dressing rooms, and the galvanized steel trough in the men's room, ended with Johnny Cash standing center stage with Maybelle Carter, Hank Snow, June Carter Cash, and fifty others singing the last number, "Will the Circle Be Unbroken." During the show most of the cast had tried to make it seem like any other night at Ryman, but many wouldn't, some couldn't. Jean Shepard, right in the middle of her song, broke into tears and ran offstage crying.

The fifty-eight-year-old Grand Ole Opry didn't actually begin at Ryman Hall, but at Studio A in the National Life Building in downtown Nashville. Then it moved to the Hillsboro Theatre, then to the Dixie Tabernacle in East Nashville, then to the War Memorial building, and finally in 1941 to Ryman, whose beginnings run like a morality play. One hot summer night in 1891, Captain Tom Ryman, a hard-nosed riverboat captain whose big loves were drinking, raising hell, and breaking up revival meetings along the Cumberland River, docked his sidewheeler in Nashville. He stormed into a tent meeting with fifteen or twenty of his

crewmen, intending to clear out Amen Row and drive the
preacher from the pulpit. But Reverend Sam P. Jones, a
leather-lunged Jesus shouter, was ready for him. As
Captain Ryman started up the sawdust trail, Jones switched
sermons and went into his favorite eulogy on Mother.
Ryman stopped. He listened. Tears came to his eyes and he
sank to the ground. When he arose, he was sanctified and
reborn. And to the amazement of the congregation, and the
agony of his crew, Tom Ryman announced that he would
dedicate the rest of his mortal life to doing the Lord's work,
and that on the very spot where he was saved he would build
the Ryman Tabernacle. Two years later the tabernacle was
dedicated to the Gospel. With a seating capacity of
thirty-three hundred, it eventually proved to be too large
for Nashville fundamentalism, and after years of serving as
a convention hall, it finally became the home of Grand Ole
Opry in 1941.

The first show at the new Opryland on March 16, 1974,
began with Acuff singing "The Wabash Cannonball." Then
he cocked his head into the mountain tenor of "You Are My
Sunshine," the song Jimmy Davis wrote and campaigned
and won two terms as governor of Louisiana on in the
fifties. Acuff himself had run for governor of Tennessee in
the forties, and Tex Ritter, singing "High Noon" and "Boll
Weevil," had tried for the U.S. Senate in 1970. Acuff lost, as
did Ritter, which may suggest something about Louisiana's
taste in music, or Tennessee politics.

Not always a singer, Roy Acuff started off as a pro
ballplayer for the New York Giants farm team, but
sunstroke ended that career. Forced to stay indoors, he
began to learn the fiddle. After traveling as a singer, picker,
and comic with Dr. Howar's Medicine Show, he organized
his own band, the Crazy Tennesseans, but "Judge" George
D. Hay, who ran the Opry at that time, told him the name
slurred the state, so he changed it to the Smoky Mountain

Boys, which it's been since 1938. For the past forty-five years, Roy Acuff and his sidemen have been playing at the Opry, touring the high schools of the state, the state fairs of the country, and the coliseums of the world. He is very honest about his talent. "I think I brought a different voice to the Opry," he recalled for Jack Hurst, author of *Nashville's Grand Old Opry.* "Most of the people back then were crooners. They sang soft; and they sang harmony, where I would just open my mouth and fill my lungs with air, and let it go with force. . . . I didn't realize how different my singing was from the rest until my mail started coming in. The letters I got would mention how clear I was coming through and how distinct my voice was and how they could understand my words." Hurst explained that, "the mechanical equipment available was too primitive to be able to transmit a very clear sound from the undisciplined live show. In the din, Acuff's brief and impassioned solo spots stood out like gun shots at midnight."

Roy Acuff once told me why he sang the same songs over and over and over again. He dodged the question at first. "You know, sometimes I'll be singing along, like on 'The Great Speckled Bird,' and if I get the right feeling going I'll almost cry. That's the kind of song you can sing every week for forty years, and each time you go at it, it's a little different. It's from Jeremiah, twelfth chapter, ninth verse." But then he leaned forward and handled the question beautifully: "Of course, you're right I got me a problem now, and there just ain't no way out of it. People say, all old Roy ever sings is 'The Great Speckled Bird' and 'The Wabash Cannonball.' . . . Lot of them think that's all I know. But you know something? There ain't a day that goes by that some fellow doesn't come in here and say, 'Roy, me and the wife's been listening to the Opry for thirty years, and this is our first time here. Do me a favor, Roy. It's her birthday, and we done drove all the way down from Wisconsin. How about playing 'The Wabash Cannonball?' " And Roy shook his head. "Now tell me, how'm I going to turn my back on something like that?"

Garrison Keillor, a disc jockey out of St. Paul who covered the opening for *The New Yorker* magazine, had decided he couldn't bear to hear the old music he was raised on played in the new auditorium. He didn't want to sit in the "specially designed contoured pew-type benches covered in burnt orange colored carpeting," or to lay eyes on this "vibrant and viable building that conveys a feeling of intimacy, informality, warmth, and charm . . . yet contains the ultimate in modern electronics, acoustics, lighting, and audio-visual equipment," all as described in an Opryland brochure. Listening to the show on his radio in a downtown motel, he writes that he closed his eyes. "I could see the stage as clearly as when I was a kid lying in front of our giant Zenith console. I'd seen a photograph of the Opry stage in a magazine back then, and believe me, one is all you need." He listened to most of the show: "And then — then — the moment I'd been waiting for. Sam and Kirk McGee from sunny Tennessee played 'San Antonio Rose.' It was the acoustic moment when the skies cleared and the weeping steels were silent, and out of the clear blue came a little ole guitar duet. Stunning and simple, and so good after all the *sound* I'd heard that week — the sweetest 'Rose' this side of Texas. I turned out the light, turned off the radio, and went to sleep on it. In the morning, the radio was on the floor, its plastic cover cracked. I believe it would still work, but I will never play it again. It is my only Opry souvenir. Inside it the McGee Brothers are still picking and will forever, Minnie Pearl cackles, the Crooks are dancing, Jim and Jesse ascend into heavenly harmony, and the great Acuff rides the Wabash Cannonball to the lakes of Minnesota, where the rippling waters fall."

Despite the controversy over the old and the new auditoriums and the fact that more than two million of the faithful drive their lives out (average distance four hundred and seventy miles one-way to come to Nashville) every year to be with the stars and tour the homes and buy the souvenirs, and that another twenty million see the Opry on syndicated TV, the show, regardless of its trappings, began as a radio program and is still conducted like one. It's been describd as "organized chaos," with groups tuning up, friends visiting friends, agents arranging dates, songwriters plugging songs, and an occasional subpoena server standing in the wings waiting for the star to finish to get him back on his alimony payments. But while it's bedlam onstage, the only sound that goes out to the audience and the radio listeners is the sound from the microphones up front and center stage.

While there are several versions of the program's exact birthday, the consensus seems to be that it first took to the air on November 28, 1925, at the National Life and Accident Insurance Company's station WSM (We Shield Millions). The story runs how Uncle Jimmy Thompson, an eighty-year-old dirt farmer, was introduced by Judge Hay, the announcer and originator of the show, and how the old gentleman claimed he knew more than one thousand fiddle songs. After his hour was up he complained, "Fiddlesticks! A man can't get warmed up in no one hour. This show has got to be longer." The show became longer, much longer, and finally expanded to four hours on Friday and four on Saturday, which brings it in as not only the world's oldest radio program, but also its longest.

Judge Hay was responsible for its name. He opened the program one night following Walter Damrosch's "Music Appreciation Hour" from New York City. "Well, folks," he said, "for the past hour we have been listening to music taken largely from Grand Opera, but from now on we will present the Grand Ole Opry. . . ." The name stuck, the show grew, and today it is broadcast and relayed to every state in the country.

When Uncle Jimmy Thompson requested that they make the show longer for him, he had no idea of the competition that was waiting in the wings. Such high-powered groups as the Possum Hunters; the Crook Brothers, with Sam and Kirk McGee; the Gulley Jumpers; and the Fruit Jar Drinkers leaped onto the stage and stayed for twenty, thirty, forty years. The Fruit Jar Drinkers, the Crook Brothers, and Sam and Kirk McGee are still with us. But the big star in the first fifteen years was the banjo-playing, singing, dancing jokester, the Dixie Dew Drop, Uncle Dave Macon. He was introduced as the "struttingest strutter that ever strutted a strut with a banjo or guitar," and his "Turkey in the Straw," "Sugar Walks Down the Street," "Ain't Going to Rain No More," and "Go Away, Mule" would set the whole audience to stomping and screaming. Uncle Dave's following was enormous. Fred Ritchie, who died in the electric chair at the Tennessee State Prison on Tuesday, August 10, 1937, for slaying his wife, had warden Joe Pope call up WSM the preceding Saturday night. This was Ritchie's last chance to hear the Grand Ole Opry and he had only one final request: he wanted Uncle Dave Macon to play "When I Take My Vacation in Heaven." Uncle Dave didn't let him down.

I once asked Grandpa Jones, a singer and comic for Martha White Flour on the Opry, if he had heard a recent song. His reply was candid: "What's it the tune to?" Country music writers have always allowed their lyrics to override the melody, and when a song's lyrics are good enough, no one complains. The seventies hit "I Didn't Know God Made Honky Tonk Angels" sounds (because it is exactly) the same as Acuff's "The Great Speckled Bird," which sounds (because it is exactly) the same as A. P. Carter's "I'm Thinking Tonight of My Blue Eyes." But then, a lot of songs go back to A. P. Carter and the Carter Family. Little has been written about the man who probably had more

influence on country music than anyone else, Alvin
Pleasant ("A. P.") Carter. In July of 1927, one Ezra Carter
forbade his wife Maybelle to accompany A. P. and his wife
Sara, who was Maybelle's cousin, into Bristol, Virginia, for a
recording session. A. P. had contacted Ralph S. Peer to
audition for a tryout. The money was to have been fifty
dollars per song; there was no guarantee of even doing one.
But Ezra told Maybelle the twenty-five miles was too far and
that there was too much to do around the house. A. P.
finally volunteered that he would clear out a patch of weeds
from Ezra's yard if he would let her go, and Ezra gave in. A.
P., Sara, and Maybelle loaded up their Model-A Ford with
instruments, and with Gladys Carter as a baby-sitter and
Baby Joe, who was still being breast-fed by Sara, they set out
for the twenty-five mile ride to Bristol. The rest is history.
With Sara's great voice and Maybelle's guitar and autoharp
virtuosity and A. P., who did the harmony and "worked up"
the songs, they were an immediate hit. Within a year they
had recorded songs that will be with us forever: "Wildwood
Flower," "John Hardy," "Forsaken Love," "Diamond in the
Rough," "Foggy Mountain Top," and on and on. Back
home in the Clinch Mountain Valley, they continued
playing at the high schools and the churches, and A. P.,
always the organizer, tacked up posters on the pine trees:
"Look! Victor artists A. P. Carter and the Carter Family will
give a musical program at Elm Hill School August 10th. . . .
This program is morally good. Twenty-five cents adults . . .
fifteen cents children."

The Carters are virtually unique in country music in that,
unlike other groups who try to find out what the public
wants, or what will sell, they stuck to what they knew and
what they loved. Close harmony became their trademark.

The Carters' most famous song is "Wildwood Flower,"
and many of its rhythms and phrasings can be found
running through most of their music. Every few years a

songwriter tries to set new lyrics to "Wildwood Flower," but the Carter arrangement is too formidable and too familiar, and the public quickly rejects it. Even Woody Guthrie tried changing it to "Reuben James," but "Wildwood Flower," which is considered the national anthem of Nashville, won out, and "Reuben James" is rarely heard these days. Another Carter song that Guthrie reworked was "Little Darling Pal of Mine." He rewrote the lyrics, and called it "This Land Is Your Land." A. P. Carter, probably knowing how fast his favorite lyrics were being changed and forgotten, saved his favorite song title for his tombstone. In 1960 he was buried in Maces Springs, Virginia; the legend under his name and dates is the simple and straightforward "Keep on the Sunny Side." Maybelle Carter's daughter June having married Johnny Cash, the Cash-Carter line may produce great music forever.

Popular music in the twenties was heading in a dozen directions at once. And even in the Appalachians, stretching from West Virginia to South Carolina — where they were still reading the Bible by kerosene light and playing hymns and ballads — radio and the recording industry soon spawned a different kind of country music. People now wanted more than Uncle Jimmy Thompson sawing away on "Old Zip Coon" and "Down Yonder;" they wanted voices they could hear and words they could follow. Many wanted the songs and singers they'd seen on the medicine shows that had rolled through their small towns, and many wanted the music of Jimmie Rodgers.

The story of Jimmie Rodgers has become a country legend. Born in Meridian, Mississippi, on September 8, 1897, he left school at fourteen to work full time as a water carrier on the railroad. Later the gandy dancers' ringing lines would find their way into his music: "Hey, little water boy, bring that water round. / If you don't like your job, put

that water bucket down." Most of Rodgers' adult life was
spent on the railroads of Mississippi and Texas, but in 1923
he tried the medicine-show business. Blacking his face, he
set out with a road show as a singer. He was a born
entertainer, and with the money he made, he invested in his
own "Hawaiian Tent Show" and made his bid for the big
money. But a high wind blew the tent down, and in a matter
of hours he lost everything he had. Forced to pawn his
banjo to get back to Carrie, his wife in Meridian, he arrived
in time for the funeral of his six-month-old daughter, June
Rebecca. One year later, broke and back on the railroad, he
discovered he had tuberculosis, and spent the next three
months in a charity hospital. Tuberculosis forced him
finally to quit the railroad at twenty-nine, and he decided to
make his living doing what he loved best, writing music and
playing it.

As Jimmie Rodgers' health failed, he traveled more,
wrote more, and with the knowledge of having only a few
more years left, began drinking hard and living as fast as he
could. On August 4, 1927, he got his big break. On the
Tennessee side of State Street in Bristol, Ralph S. Peer, who
a month before had recorded the Carter Family, recorded
the first Jimmie Rodgers record. It was an instant sensation,
and in the next few years he was to record one hundred and
eleven more songs, most of them his own: "I'm Lonely and
Blue," "Way Out on the Mountain," "Freight Train Blues,"
"Muleskinner Blues," and his famous "*T* for *T*exas, *T* for
*T*ennessee, / *T* for *T*helma, that gal that made a wreck out of
me." His success, with its built-in sense of self-destruction,
fed his popularity. He was living the wild and doomed life
his fans identified with.

Rodgers' first hits featured his famous "Blue Yodel," and
when he hit the big time, he built himself a mansion in
Kerrville, Texas, and called it Blue Yodeler's Paradise. In
his song "Jimmie the Kid," he tells much of his own story:

"I'll tell you a story about Jimmie the Kid, / A brakeman you all know. He shoveled coal / On the T & N & P.O. . . ." The list of railroads goes on, along with his failures and his successes and his great pride in Carrie, his daughter Anita, and his Blue Yodeler's Paradise.

For six years Jimmie Rodgers recorded and toured the country appearing with such stars as Gene Austin and Will Rodgers, and as the tuberculosis weakened him, he seemed to work harder. Maybelle Carter recalled recording with him a year before his death. "I played [guitar] for him. . . . He wasn't able to play . . . he was that sick. . . . I had to play like him, you know, so everybody would think it was him. But it was me."

In April, 1933, Jimmie Rodgers knew the end was in sight. In New York for a recording session, he rested between takes on a cot set up in the studio. The last twelve songs recorded there were to provide for Carrie and Anita. On May 25, on a sightseeing trip to Coney Island, he began hemorrhaging, and late the next day at the Taft Hotel he died at the age of thirty-six.

Talents like Jimmie Rodgers — and jazz stars Billie Holliday and Charlie Parker — in reaching for the better tunes, the fresher licks, and the newer sounds, keep stepping up the pace until they are producing more songs, more music, and more poetry in one year than the rest of us do in a lifetime. But they pay a fierce price, fueling their talent with whiskey, pills, and running around until it breaks them.

It is as if Hank Williams, who was born in Georgiana, Alabama, in 1923 and grew up selling peanuts and shining shoes, had read the book on Jimmie Rodgers and then set out to follow the same wild and careening trail. At twenty-six, after a wretched life filled with rejection, poverty, and living up to his reputation for being a drunk, he finally got a chance on the Opry. His first song was his own "Lovesick Blues," which is still one of the toughest songs around. The crowd forced him to sing six encores and were standing on their feet screaming for more when Red Foley, the master of ceremonies, finally had to tell them there were other singers on the show, and they had his solemn promise that they would be seeing a lot more of Mr. Hank Williams.

Williams' life held a raw and wild mixture of talent and unhappiness, and the problems that locked themselves onto him were so great that the only wonder is he managed to hang on as long as he did. By 1952, three years after singing "Lovesick Blues" and after making five hundred thousand dollars and writing such songs as "Cold, Cold Heart," "I'm So Lonesome I Could Cry," "Jambalaya," "Your Cheatin' Heart," "I Saw the Light," "Honky Tonkin'," and "I'll Never Get Out of This World Alive," the bottom began to come out. He was showing up for concerts drunk or not showing up at all. In the same year in which he and his first wife were divorced, he was suspended from the Grand Ole Opry for being too drunk to perform. Hank Williams found a new wife, but now almost broke, he was forced to restage the marriage for money in a Shreveport, Louisiana, theater: two shows, an afternoon "rehearsal," and an evening ceremony. Williams' health, like Rodgers', was beginning to go, and then, in typical country music style, instead of checking into a hospital or seeing a real doctor, he took his sickness to a quack with a faked medical certificate. Hank Williams by this time had only one ambition, to be allowed back on the stage of his beloved Grand Ole Opry. He might have made it, but on a long drive from Montgomery to Canton, Ohio, to play a date on New Year's Day, 1954, he died of heart failure, perhaps brought on by an overdose of drugs. He was twenty-nine. Commerce goes on; today in Nashville the green Cadillac he died in is on exhibit, and for twelve dollars I was offered what was claimed to be the needle he OD'd on, set in Lucite.

Country music, which has been defined to death, resists every classification except Kris Kristofferson's "If it sounds country, man, it's country." It is a blend of British balladry, American folk, Protestant hymns, Southern white theme, and black blues. "Sometimes the music is called 'hillbilly music,' " writes novelist Charles Portis, "which is only half accurate, because the Southern lowlands have contributed just as much as the hill folks, perhaps more; and sometimes 'country and western,' which is misleading because much of it reflects the culture west of Abilene, Texas, and tends to be pretty thin stuff. 'Southern-white working-class music' would never do as a tag. But that's what it is."

Perhaps it's even simpler than that. Mastering a guitar or banjo lick or working out a new style, as in the case of the Carter Family or Jimmie Rodgers or Hank Williams, may very well come as a relief from the tension and the boredom of the day's work. Earl Scruggs, who popularized the three-finger banjo-picking style, said it cleanly, "I taught myself. We were on the farm and it was in the winter. I didn't have anything else to do."

Merle Travis, who wrote "Sixteen Tons," "Smoke, Smoke, Smoke That Cigarette," "Dark as a Dungeon," and originated a whole new method of guitar picking — which he describes as splitting his left hand in half while he plays the bass with his thumb — once said, "There is always a better guitar player on down the road. Always." The new musician gets richer tones, faster runs, and comes up with new chords, and people gather around and listen. Then someone else picks it up, and then it travels. It's easy to see how pickers can keep doing showboat runs and fast fret patterns on the back porch after work and eventually figure out a whole new sound, a whole new technique, from simply trying to get ready for the new player who's just ridden into town. A Grand Ole Opry favorite, "The Orange Blossom Special," which no one wrote and everybody wrote, has a rich structure, much like jazz, which has evolved out of thousands of hours of fiddle and guitar players trying to out-perform one another. Listen to the song and watch for the setup which allows the soloists to step forward and do their stuff and then sit back down and wait to do it again. Listen also for the incredible accumulation that sets the stage for the best fiddler in the area and challenges him to try and cut it.

Travis, who is always looking for that phantom lick out there in the dark beyond his talent, told me about the competition and the search. Much of it is done under the guise of general horsing around, but the competition is there. "This old boy came to my dressing room down in Waco, Texas, with a sheet of music, wanting to know how I fretted a double B chord. I said, 'A double B?' Yeah, that fool thought B-flat was a double B. Called it big B and little B. Well, I asked him if his fingers were limber, and he wiggled them around and told me he could reach and hold anything. Right there was where he made his mistake. I wound that rascal around that guitar neck like a pea vine running through a cyclone fence. I had him put a finger on four places an octopus couldn't reach, and I said, 'You got it.' That old boy was holding on, sweating bullets, and his hand was so cramped up and stretched out so far it was throbbing. He said, 'Yessir, I got her. I got her. But she's slipping. . . . It's going to take some strong practice to do this one. But listen, I sure appreciate this.' "

There is a lyric in the old song "On Top of Old Smokey" that runs: "He'll tell you more lies, / Than the crossties on the railroad, / Or the stars in the skies." Somehow that horizon, out where the railroad and the clustering stars come together, captures the feelings that country music tries to touch; the sadness, the trouble, and the neon-lit, lonesome beauty of it all. Songs like Loretta Lynn's "Blue Kentucky Girl;" Jimmie Rodgers' "Way Out on the Mountain;" Hank Williams' "I'm So Lonesome I Could

Cry;" Patsy Cline's "I Fall to Pieces;" Emmylou Harris' "Till I Gain Control Again;" and Willie Nelson's "Blue Eyes Crying in the Rain," shimmer with this unexplainable quality and, as far as a lot of us are concerned, stand a good chance of maybe lasting forever.

While I was in Nashville the last time, I walked through old Ryman, trying to remember my favorite performance. The church pews are still slick from the years of wear since Captain Tom Ryman had them carved for Reverend Jones, and the sunlight streaming through the high and pointed red, yellow, and blue tabernacle windows still washes colors over the Confederate Gallery, the front rows, and across the big stage. The watchman's dog was sleeping in the center aisle, and as I moved around him, the old wooden floor creaked. Thinking back, it wasn't hard to remember one night back in the sixties when Lester Flatt and Earl Scruggs were riding together on the Martha White portion of the show. I was sitting in the orchestra in the middle of the fried chicken, the sausage biscuits, the beer. I took no notes that night because I needed none. But later I jotted down some at the Alamo Plaza and still later they found their way into a novel I was working on. While this description doesn't catch the music, because I know of no way to do that, it does point to it as it goes winging by, which may be all we can ever do.

"Flatt and Scruggs and The Foggy Mountain Boys came on like race horses, steel sharp and as right as railroad spikes. The high-pitched banjo crawled up on top, the low fiddle growl held at the side, while the steady driving dobro underneath pushed it all together and straight out at us. It curled and skipped, danced and broke and raced forward, ricocheting off sheet metal onto some wilder level where heat lightning flashed and forked and waited. The Foggy Mountain Boys held the frenzied bridge for eight straight bars, and Earl Scruggs tipped his white hat and stepped in tight. The rest backed. He came on somber-faced, expressionless, placid, and picking like a madman. High, shrill, and quick as a lizard. His jaw was set and his eyes were riveted to the twin spider hands as his ten fingers with twenty different things to do walked back and forth on the ebony-black and mother-of-pearl five string frets. He went to the top of where he was going, held it, and then slid down in a machine-gun run of sharp C, G, and A notes, bowed quickly and stepped back as his partner, Lester Flatt, his guitar up high with the box to his ear, moved in. He sang with his eyes closed, his head cocked for range, and threw out his nasal, perfect tones in a short sowbelly arc that rose and fell, gathering in all the mountain folds, wood smoke, and purple twilights of the Cumberlands. He was unconscious of the crowd and the back-up men, of himself. He heard only the music which raised him up high on his toes and twisted him around until his jaw was pointing to the top of the long curved ceiling. No one in the crowd spoke, coughed, or shifted. They strained forward, not wanting to miss a beat, a sound, a flash. It was an old Carter song, 'I Still Think the Good Things Outweigh the Bad.' It wasn't gospel, but as the words hung in the heat and the hundred-year-old oak of Ryman, it was gospel for Lester Flatt. The back-up men moved in to pick him up. They were dark-eyed and haunted-looking under their big shadow-throwing hats. Too many years and nights on the road had ground them down, but it had sharpened them and their music into the close-grained group they were. They heard each other and they listened. They blocked for one another and dovetailed in right, building, breaking, and backing up with tight close counterpoints. The fiddle player swooped in with wild slides and dips, stops, double stops, and high, close, screech work at the top of the neck. They peaked and held, and then easing off, they stepped

aside as Mister Earl Scruggs moved back in. He cranked the
D tuner down, then up on the peg head and slicing into a
fresh key brought the house down with his blinding,
showering finish. The crowd rose shouting, whistling, and
stomping, and throwing their chicken boxes in the air. And
with the flash bulbs exploding from every angle, I'm here to
tell you that I was right there in the middle and making
more noise than anyone."

Charleston's
Oldest Foursome

I
T WAS MIDNIGHT and Bert Seagrave, the
club pro at Charleston Golf and Driving,
was pounding on Judge Farnsworth's door. As the lights
came on, he glanced up at the bright stars and the full
moon. At least it would be pleasant for the Governor's Cup
— no rain, very little wind. Farnsworth was cursing in the
foyer. "Who in hell's here at this damnable hour?"

Bert whipped his cap off as the big door swung open. "It's
me, sir." Farnsworth was nearsighted and moved in close.
"Young Seagrave?"

"Yessir." Bert was fifty-eight and had risen to club
professional through the junior, the senior, and the
tenured caddy ranks. "I'm sorry, sir, but the Steering
Committee just adjourned. They asked me to bring you the
minutes."

"Oh, yes, yes. I forgot. Come in, come in. You look like
you could use a drink."

Seagrave hesitated. At Charleston Golf and Driving he
took his meals with the caddies and used the tradesman's
entrance. "But, sir."

"It's all right, Seagrave. Come in, man. Come in."

Farnsworth poured the brandy and dropped into his extra wide, extra deep leather chair. The Steering Committee had been in session since seven. Suddenly, his face flushed, his hands were trembling.

Bert started. "Are you all right, sir?"

"This is outrageous!" He shook the report in the air. "Have you read this muck?"

"Oh, no, sir."

Farnsworth glared at Seagrave. "Your father would spin in his grave if he heard this. Listen: 'Resolved; in view of the plethora. . . .' " Farnsworth's legal lip curled back in disgust. "Plethora, now there's a word for you." He continued, " '. . . of complaints about the slow playing of Messrs. Farnsworth, Finlay, Laborde, and Biddle, we must insist that they use golf carts in the Governor's Cup or, regrettably, they will not be permitted to play.' "

Bert hesitated. "But you won't be withdrawing, sir?"

"Never! We will never withdraw." He studied the moisture in the brandy snifter. "This is a terrible day, Stanley."

"It's Bert, sir. My father was Stanley."

"Oh, yes, of course. This will go down hard on Laborde and Biddle. God knows how I'll break the news to old Finlay."

"It might be easier, sir, if I told him. After all, I'm the professional and. . . ."

"Nonsense, Seagrave, nonsense. This is my job."

It was morning, and the gold and maroon Governor's Cup banner was stretched across the first tee, and tournament flags were flying. Farnsworth, Finlay, Laborde, and Biddle teed off at nine, and the gallery and the waiting foursomes gave them a round of applause as they climbed into the golf carts and headed out. Finlay tipped his hat. Laborde and Biddle, who had clients in the crowd, waved. Farnsworth merely nodded, as he gloomily steered the cart down the middle of the fairway. Finlay, delighted with his one hundred and thirty-yard drive, was lighting up his Prince Albert pipe. "Old sport, I had no idea these machines were this comfortable. I can hardly hear the motor." Farnsworth stopped at Finlay's ball and looked back at the foursome warming up on the tee behind them. "You'll try and move along today, won't you?"

Finlay balanced his pipe on the drink holder. "Right, I'll take just one practice swing." With a handicap of thirty-nine, Finlay was nicknamed the Deerstalker because of his fore and aft Sherlock Holmes cap and his excruciating deliberations on the greens. He had been slow-timed by the Steering Committee at four minutes and fifty seconds on a single five-foot putt, and was constantly being posted on the bulletin board. He lined up an imaginary ball and flexed his knees. Finlay's trembling address and slow motion takeaway have been compared to the hypnotic movement of the praying mantis, and in the Christmas Follies he has won the dubious first prize for the "Golfer Who Could Be Recognized From the Greatest Distance." Finally, he swung. "Ah, nice. Nice." He paused and a faint smile softened his thin lips. "I think I'll take just one more."

While Laborde and Biddle had incurable slices and spent their time combing the weeds beyond the white stakes and holding branches back for one another, Farnsworth and Finlay often would be found in the fairway. The judge, who had the low handicap in the foursome, twenty-eight, was short with a massive waist, a flat plunging swing, and a built-in hook. The father Stanley and the son Bert had instructed him to forget his legs and his hips and, at the top, to simply concentrate on hitching his stomach out of the way. On the rare occasion when he was able to follow this schizophrenic procedure and swing upright, he would surprise himself with a one hundred and fifty-yarder down the center.

One would think that Laborde and Biddle, who shared a highly successful Broad Street brokerage as well as the same malady, the whistling slice, would have in some way been able to assist one another. But, such was not the case. A. J. Poindexter in his splendid journal, *The Green Fairway*, reminds us, "As the lover views the beloved through ruby-shaded lenses, so the golfer observes his own game; alas, clear vision and logic seldom enter." In any event, Laborde and Biddle had matching thirty handicaps, and where Laborde drove, so drove Biddle. Today's shots were so close that a hand towel from a competent manufacturer could easily have covered the pair. So while we see Farnsworth and Finlay slowly proceeding up the middle of the fairway, Laborde and Biddle are holding back the magnolia branches for one another and chipping out safety shots in preparation for their next slices, that will take them back again.

As a serious scholar of golf, you may ask how this strange friendship has lasted for more than forty years. To this there is a simple answer. While Farnsworth will vary from the middle to the hard left and Finlay will keep short and down the middle, Laborde and Biddle will go to the right and remain to the right. It then follows that any disputes beginning at the tee (i.e., scores, honors, rules, slander) normally will be forgotten during the long interim to the green. From green to tee, however, is quite another story, and the mechanics here are worth describing. Farnsworth, Laborde, and Biddle, being unable to speed up Finlay on the putting surface, have long ago worked out a plan of action, which is carefully and scrupulously followed. Finlay, whether he is one foot from the cup or sixty, remains completely off the green until the others have putted.

Then, after they hole out, they leave him to his elaborate scanning and plumb-bobbing and head for the next tee. By doing this, they avoid the nerve-racking waits and spare themselves the howls and protestations from the unfortunate foursomes playing behind. Indeed, the only time they are together is on the tee and at the halfway house.

And so, as the Charleston Golf and Driving Seventy-Third Governor's Cup opens, with the victorious foursome looking forward to receiving not only the sterling trophy and the customary magnum of champagne, but also the honor of serving as Steering Committee for the following year, we might pause and gaze for a moment at the plaque of winners and runner-ups in the wainscoted club room. Farnsworth, Finley, Laborde, and Biddle are, of course, absent on the bronze above us, but here below in the big leather-and-brass bound book of records we find their bold signatures, and our hearts must surely soften. For their thirty-four consecutive entries, their singular reward has been a contested tie for ninth in the year the great general came to office and led the republic through the dark days of the fifties. While many would scoff at placing ninth, for this foursome, it must be said, it was the equivalent of scaling the Matterhorn. In short, nothing would please them more than replaying that same game in that memorable year. But facts, as grim as they often may be, have to be faced. The winning foursome for the past five years and the favorites for today, Messrs. Colbert, Stagg, Huddelston, and Van Rooten, who are also the Steering Committee, were auctioned off in the Calcutta for twenty-two hundred dollars. The bidding for Farnsworth, Finlay, Laborde, and Biddle started at twenty dollars and promptly stopped.

And so, leaving the oak-paneled room with the Tiffany lamps and the leaded windows, and joining our foursome on the second tee, we note that Farnsworth's look is one of composed dissatisfaction. The first hole was uneventful—a six for Farnsworth and a brace of eights for Laborde and Biddle. They have left Finlay on the green microscopically surveying an eighteen-footer for a nine. The second hole, a right-to-left dogleg, has a lily pond forty yards beyond the right rough, so far out of play that it doesn't appear on the course map on the back of the card. It is into this that Laborde and Biddle plunge. Farnsworth shakes his head in disbelief and levers a duck hook into the left rough as Finlay arrives with the news that he has four-putted for a twelve. Then after two torturously long practice swings, he shanks a sixty-degree shot in with Laborde and Biddle. Suddenly, Farnsworth is out of the cart. His hands are raised, as if he's stopping traffic. "Hold it! Let's get a hold of ourselves. It's these carts. You're letting them rush you. Now slow it down. Slow it down and think."

Everyone agreed and everyone solemnly promised to ignore the carts and play their old game. And then everyone, including Farnsworth, dubbed their next shot. Five shots later, only Farnsworth was on the green. Laborde and Biddle had caught the right trap, and Finlay had skulled onto the back apron in nine. Miraculously, Farnsworth saved the hole with a twenty-foot slider for a seven and a net bogie.

Three holes later, Farnsworth clearly saw the handwriting on the wall — unless he did something drastic and something soon, they would probably win another two-inch-high booby-prize trophy with the withering inscription, "Better luck next time, only not here, please."

He cleared his head, as he had done a thousand times on the judicial bench, and slowly arranged the facts. Being snatched forward by the hair-trigger accelerator and slammed back when he braked had rattled him. Instead of being helpful, as he often was, to Laborde and Biddle, his irritation had unnerved them and they were slicing deeper than he had ever seen. And possibly — perhaps subconsciously, but possibly, nevertheless — they were slicing deeper in a desperate attempt to avoid him. And then he looked at Finlay, and couldn't believe he had been so blind. His deerstalker cap was on at an absurd angle and his shirttail was out. The old dodger, who was always impeccable and a model of golfing dress, was wearing his trousers four inches lower than Farnsworth had ever seen them, and his whole appearance was that of a badly-tied angler's fly. Farnsworth knew it was the cart. The climbing in, the chilling ride, and the sudden stops and starts were unraveling him and wearing him down. Worst of all, his confidence was gone, and a new tuning-fork tremble had insinuated itself into his raised elbows at the top of his swing.

On the next tee, Farnsworth straightened Finlay's cap and made him arrange his trousers. Then he announced a new game plan: He, Laborde, and Biddle would ride; Finlay would walk.

When the foursome behind saw Finlay walking, they set up a chorused howl that hung in the air a full thirty seconds. Farnsworth ignored them. Finlay didn't hear them and on the next shot surprised everyone, including himself, with a one hundred and twenty-yard eleven-wood down the center. And then, as the foursome took up the plaintive cry, "No, Finlay, no! Use the cart!" and was joined in turn by still another foursome, Finlay moved slowly up the fairway.

Farnsworth, seeing Finlay's improvement, rode easier and soon was neatly hitching his stomach out of the way and swinging upright. He hit two in a row down the middle. After his third, which was stiff to the pin, he gazed over at Laborde and Biddle with a new light gleaming in his eyes. Poindexter has pondered on this exotic phenomenon: "One may take the lowliest forty handicapper, who in the course of a full lifetime will possibly break one hundred two, or at best three, times and watch him hit two long woods back-to-back and then wedge up for his par. This same miscreant, who normally cannot put seven words together in a simple declarative sentence, between the green he has left and the tee he is heading for, will become a veritable fount of golfing advice and Royal and Ancient Wisdom. Fortunately, he very soon will come a cropper and return to his regular game and the meeching silence that blessedly goes with it."

And so it went with Farnsworth. Having solved Finlay's problem and seemingly his own, he took on the challenge of Laborde and Biddle. Whisking across the fairway and into the light woods, he followed them like a stalking hunter. Finally, when Laborde was alone, he closed in. "Hugo, I want you to do me a favor."

"Sure, Gene, anything."

Farnsworth was out of the car with his five iron. He demonstrated. "I want you to close the face, like this."

Laborde, a timid man who would say yes to anything, did so. "Jesus, Gene, I can read it."

"Fine, that's what you want."

"This is crazy." He swung and the ball slammed into Farnsworth's cart. Farnsworth was on him like a hawk. "Fine, Hugo! Fine. Now do it again." This time the ball duck-hooked across the fairway. Laborde grinned. "Hey! I'll take that."

"Marvelous, Hugo. Marvelous."

Biddle, deep in the woods, saw Farnsworth's eyes shining as the cart came closer.

"Hold it, Gene. No instructions. O.K.?"

"But look what I did for Hugo. I just don't want us finishing last again."

"Just leave me alone. I've got enough troubles."

"O.K., Andrew, I'm only trying to be helpful." He flipped the reverse switch and backed out of the woods.

Slowly, ever so slowly, the holes rolled by. The foursomes

behind were howling and growing mutinous, but Finlay would not be rushed. By the time the foursome reached the ninth tee, the Seventy-Third Governor's Cup was in shambles. Two foursomes had withdrawn, and five others had lodged grievance action complaints. With Finlay walking and Farnsworth motoring back and forth across the fairway and giving instructions to Laborde, and stalking Biddle, and then attending to his own game, the first eight holes had taken more than four hours. The eighteen would be well over eight hours, and while they would finish before dark, the foursomes behind them would never make it. Twenty members, with a signed petition, met them at the halfway house demanding that they leave the carts and use caddies, or withdraw and be driven in in the club's limousine. But Farnsworth, knowing he needed the carts to keep his system working, countered with a better offer. They would let the trailing foursomes play through. It was immediately accepted. As the foursomes came through, grumbling and harried from the long waits and the running battles with Finlay, they didn't mind Farnsworth peering at their score cards. And as he did, his hopes slowly began to rise; they still had an outside chance for eleventh or even tenth.

One hour later, they teed off on the one hundred and thirty-yard tenth. Finlay, with a ten wood, lofted the ball eighteen feet from the hole. This time Farnsworth, Laborde, and Biddle waited on the apron to watch the putt. Finlay's first move, a slow circling of the entire green, was followed by a careful checking of the line from the front, from the back, the right side, the left. He then went into his elaborate plumb-bobbing.

Farnsworth grimaced. "Jesus, what next?"

And then he heard what was next. Finlay was singing. "I'll take Manhattan, / The Bronx and Staten Island, too."

Farnsworth groaned.

Biddle touched his elbow. "Not so loud."

Finlay, crouching in over the ball, was timing himself with the old four/four melody. He stopped and looked over. "I didn't see you standing there."

Farnsworth smiled quickly. "We're not bothering you, are we?"

"Oh no. It's rather nice having you there. I'm hitting for the inside of the right lip. Take a look."

They all crouched and looked, and they all agreed. As Finlay plumb-bobbed one last time, he glanced over. "Laborde, you want to move the pipe? I'm catching the smoke in the corner of my eye."

Then Finlay addressed the ball and began the last chorus. As the song ended, he rocked forward and then back. His backswing was too full and the ball shot from the club face. It slammed into the back of the cup, leaped a full foot straight up in the air, and dropped back in. A sixteenth-inch off center and it would have cleared the green.

"Outstanding!" Farnsworth was shouting. "Absolutely outstanding!" He marked in the net zero and circled it as Laborde lovingly picked up the smoldering pipe and Biddle rushed over and began pounding him on his back.

The excitement continued. On the eleventh Laborde hit two long rolling hooks, reached the green in three and one-putted for a par. It was a net eagle. Farnsworth made a par on the twelfth for another eagle, and on the thirteenth, Biddle, giving in to Farnsworth's pleading to close the face, did so and wound up with a third net eagle. The fourteenth, fifteenth, and sixteenth yielded up two net birdies and a par, and Farnsworth was trembling as he whispered to Laborde. "If we can just hold it, Hugo, we're in the top ten."

Laborde was so excited he was stammering. "I know, I know. Thank God we're out of last."

Farnsworth gripped his elbow. "Not a word to Finlay, understand?"

"Absolutely."

At the seventeenth ballwasher, Farnsworth saw a cart coming up the fairway. At first he thought it was an official coming out with some trumped-up U.S.G.A. slow-play ruling that they had been disqualified. But then he saw that it was Seagrave. Everyone had finished and he had the scores on a single sheet. "Sir, you're in great shape."

After a quick calculation, Farnsworth saw it. He whispered, "Jesus! We're fifth."

Laborde and Biddle's faces drained white. They couldn't speak. Finally, Biddle whispered, "Shall we tell Finlay?"

Farnsworth said, "God, no."

The possibility of finishing fifth was too much for Farnsworth; he whiffed his tee shot and went to one knee. It was also too much for Laborde and Biddle, who quickly compounded the felony by scurrying into the loblolly pines and the rhododendron. Finlay, who was blithely innocent of the unbelievable news, stroked down the middle, and down the middle, and down the middle onto the green four feet from the cup. Farnsworth was stunned; he couldn't believe any of it, but there was Finlay again putting for still another net eagle. Once again, he was brushing down the tiniest imperfection and wiping away the slightest moisture. After the elaborate, ceremonial preparation, during which Farnsworth lit a cigarette, smoked it down to the filter, and lit another, Finlay finally croaked out the last line of an ancient sea chanty and then stroked the ball smoothly into the absolute center of the cup.

Biddle couldn't contain himself. "An eagle! My God! We're third!"

Farnsworth shouted, "Shut up!"

But Finlay had heard "third." He looked over smiling. "Third what?"

Farnsworth moved swiftly. "Your third shot, old man. We think it was your best one of the day."

Finlay cocked his head like a curious bird. "But how about my drive on ten?"

Farnsworth wrapped his arm around Finlay's shoulders. "Of course, of course. What were we thinking?"

Finlay would gladly have spent the day discussing either one of the shots, but Farnsworth keep him moving and changed the subject to the poor service in the club room.

For a one hundred and eighty-yard par three, the eighteenth at Charleston Golf and Driving is one of the hardest-finishing holes in the country. The entire carry is over water, and the ball has to be floated onto the small, camel-backed green softly, or there is very little chance of anything but disaster. Farnsworth kept drying, and drying, and re-drying his hands. But they wouldn't stay dried, and he gave up and stepped up to the ball. At the top of his swing, while concentrating on keeping his grip firm, he forgot to hitch his stomach. The ball never had a chance and, hooking out twenty yards, it plunged in. Laborde and Biddle, as if hypnotized to follow him, did so, and three sets of concentric circles were left shimmering out on the black pond. They hit again, and once again, all three splashed in. With six sets of circles crossing and re-crossing each other, Farnsworth looked sadly over at his old friend. "Finlay, are you ready?"

But Finlay, working on some delicate adjustment at the top of his swing, didn't hear him. He took another practice swing and, holding his follow-through at the top, he checked and re-checked his alignment and his hands. Then he saw Farnsworth waiting. "Sorry, Gene. I'm ready now."

Finlay, who carried fourteen custom-made woods, was on the tee with four of them. After testing the wind with a wet finger, he selected his driver. Farnsworth, desperately trying to remember if Finlay had *ever* cleared the water, was slowly realizing that he hadn't. He knew he should forget Finlay and concentrate on his own game. If he could get on in five and down in seven, or even eight, they would still be in fifth or sixth. Fifth would be wonderful. Sixth would be wonderful. Seventh, or eighth, or ninth would be wonderful.

Finlay was ready, and he stooped over with a dark, brown-stained ball. Farnsworth saw it and hurried forward. "Damn, that thing's ten years old."

"I always use old balls here."

"Well, not today." Farnsworth knelt and teed up a brand-new Titleist.

"Thanks, Gene. I guess you know what you're doing." Finlay dug in his spikes and flexed his knees deeply. Farnsworth, Laborde, and Biddle were twisting, turning, daring not to watch, daring not to not watch. Finlay adjusted his grip, rocked forward, and then rocked back. This time the swing with the trembling elbows at the top was even slower, and as it etched itself against the dark pond, he looked like an ancient professor carefully drawing a giant circle on the blackboard. The ball was badly struck and was low and doomed. But wait, it's skipping. Once! Twice! But it can't clear the lake! It can't clear the bank! It skips a third time and splashes into the edge. But then, a strange thing happens; the ball, like a mechanical mouse, has worked its way up the bank and onto the green, only forty feet from the cup.

Later, Seagrave explained that it was a rare case of delayed top spin that did it. But now, we have no time, or need, for explanations. Our foursome is racing for the green, and the gallery is racing out from the clubhouse to see the outcome. Once again, Seagrave is in Farnsworth's ear with the scores and the possibilities; if Finlay can three-putt for a four, with his three strokes they are in uncontested second place.

Farnsworth couldn't take it all in. The world was swimming before his eyes. He had to let Seagrave drive the cart, and he cautioned himself to take it easy, to calm down. But his heart was surging and pounding in his throat, and he was silently screaming, "Three putts: second place! We'll be runners-up! We'll be on the bronze!"

It would be heaven. It would be all he'd ever hoped for and yearned for and prayed for; it would be everything. He had to keep moving. He had to keep doing things. He joined Laborde on the apron. "Three putts, Hugo, and we're second. We're runners-up."

"I know. My God, I can't believe it."

"Don't let him see you smiling." He looked around. "Where's Biddle?"

"Over in the bushes. He couldn't take it. He'll be O.K. in a minute."

As Laborde left to hit his ninth shot, a small, dry voice spoke to Farnsworth. He listened closely, for it was his own. "Why can't he get down in two?" He made himself not think about it. As he closed his eyes, praying for three putts, he heard the awards presentation. "Ladies and gentlemen, I give you the runners-up in the seventy-third annual Governor's Cup, Messrs. Farnsworth, Finlay, Laborde, and Biddle." Yes, three putts would be wonderful. It would be glorious. It would be the most wonderful and glorious day in his life. But then Farnsworth's eyes narrowed and his tongue tipped lightly over his top lip, for he knew he was lying. Poindexter has waxed philosophical on this delicate subject. "One may take a man of seventy full years and return him to his twenty-fifth birthday and outfit him with a thirty-six-foot sailing sloop and place a Babylonian princess at his side, and the bounder will feel cheated if, in the silver bowl on the mahogany table before him, he cannot find the proper peppermints." In short, gentle reader, there is no such thing as enough, and in Judge Eugene Hill Farnsworth we see before us a man caught up in the full vortex of all the lust handed down to us from the days of

Adam. For the Governor's Cup championship, and a seat on the Steering Committee, and his name in bronze above the mantel, he would strike a bargain with the cloven-footed beast himself.

And so, with Farnsworth and LaBorde and Biddle and most of the active members of the club watching, Finlay begins his labors. First, he marks the ball with a dime and examines it for cuts and bruises. Finding none, he cleans it carefully. He then examines the lie. Satisfying himself that the Bermuda blades are uniform and the moisture even, he replaces the ball even more carefully. Then, bending down and remaining down to avoid getting up and bending down again, he slowly works his way along the line over the arching camel back. He is bent over so low and for so long that, from a distance, he could easily be mistaken for a man looking for a contact lens, or less charitably, a man in the painful throes of passing a stone. Following this comes the sighting from all sides. And then the song. This time it's "A Shanty in Old Shanty Town." Singing softly, he carefully places the blade in front of the ball, and then, softly singing, he carefully places it in back. And then his forehead creases deep in concentration; he has forgotten the last lines. As he frantically looks around for help, Farnsworth springs to his side with his forefinger bobbing like a metronome. His baritone voice is raised and Finlay settles down as together they harmonize:

> There's a Queen waiting there / In an old rocking chair / In a shanty in old shanty town.

As "town" rings out, Finlay waggles, Finlay swings, and Finlay strikes, and everyone's eyes are riveted on the gleaming Titleist as it begins its journey up the careening camel-back. At the crest it hesitates and almost stops. Then, as the pull of the river and running grain take over, it starts forward again. It comes off the hill gathering speed, pausing and slowing where the evening moisture has collected, and then arches out into the graceful and beautiful curve which will be etched on Farnsworth's mind forever, and goes gliding for the hole, where it suddenly vanishes like some small creature of the night. It is a birdie two, and with Finlay's three strokes, a minus one. It is an uncontested first place, an uncontested victory, and the shouts and Rebel yells from our foursome, mixed with the deep cries of pure and howling pain from the club members, can be heard all the way out to Fort Sumter.

It is now later; the champagne and the awards dinner with the trophy presentation and the taking of the Steering Committee oath are over, and we see our foursome before the blazing log under the bronze plaque that has been chalked in for the engraver — Governor's Cup Champions 1983; Farnsworth, Finlay, Laborde, Biddle. A piano player is picking out "Carolina Moon" and the aromas of Havana cigars and fine brandy are in the air. They are in the leather wing-backed chairs before the fire, and as they swirl and tip the Courvoisier, the golden light catches and shimmers in the big glasses and flickers up the wainscoting over the bronze and on up into the vaulted ceiling itself. But hark, what do we hear? It is Farnsworth's deep voice, and he is reading from the venerable Poindexter. " 'I can easily imagine the stalwart Ted Ray and the impeccable Sir Henry Vardon appearing today on the first tee at Charleston Golf and Driving in knickers, vest, and checkered socks, and feeling as comfortable as they did when they played here in the famous Member-Guest of '08.' " Farnsworth is skipping ahead. "Ah yes, here, here it is." He continues, " 'If it could be said of any course, it would have to be said that here, without any doubt, is the perfect and the ultimate haven for the Royal and the Ancient.' " Farnsworth clears his throat. "Gentlemen of the Steering Committee, this is the kind of course we must have."

"Hear, hear!"

More drinks are poured, and the plans are now being made. It is, of course, a happy moment, a great moment, and while we cannot pick out individual voices, there is no need, for now at least, they are one. "Yes, we'll keep the carts. After all, we're not getting any younger."

"Women, yes. We'll have to give in on that. But only on Sundays. And only after four."

"And I say no more Bermuda shorts, even with the long socks. Maybe we can negotiate on neckties, but then we can hold the line and insist on long sleeves."

"Hear, hear!"

"And the trap on three?"

"We'll take it out."

"And I've always thought the course played better when it was down around fifty-two hundred."

"Yes, gentlemen, I see a good year coming. A very, very good year. More brandy, gentlemen? Biddle, give Finlay a nudge there, like a good fellow."

Leroy 'Satchel' Paige

S ATCHEL PAIGE?" I was talking to a housekeeper on Charles Street in New York City in 1965. "Why, I saw him play up at the Polo Grounds forty years ago. Lord, that man must be eighty now."

A bootblack near the Time-Life Building: "I played against him in the thirties. Let's see, I'm sixty-four, and he's older than me."

A purchasing agent in Hoboken: "If you see him, tell him you met someone who got a hit off him. Not many can say that. I played against him back in the early thirties when he brought his Kansas City Monarchs into Newark."

When death finally caught Leroy "Satchel" Paige on June 8, 1982, the wire service obituary listed his age at "75 or so." No one knew for sure.

Some people swore that Satchel was well over eighty years old, and a multimillionaire. Others said he was just fifty, stone broke, and living in South America. One "knew" for a fact that he was still in Cuba and pitching shut-out ball.

They all had one thing in common: They claimed to know him personally.

I met Satch for a beer in the "Rythm Room" of the Twilight Zone Bowling Alley in Kansas City, Missouri, in the summer of '65. A long horseshoe bar backed up with a big mirror was in the front. Booths and tables lined the walls, and a red-and-blue jukebox on the side never stopped playing. The bowling alleys were in the rear. Three drinking men were arguing about what round Ezzard Charles stopped Joe Louis. The bartender shouted, "Call the Man. Here's a dime. Call the *Star* and I'll bet you a hundred dollars he says it was the twelfth." The argument stopped while one of the men went to a pay telephone.

Satch and I were having a beer in one of the front booths. The first thing he told me was that Charles had stopped Louis in the twelfth round. Satchel Paige didn't walk or talk or think or pitch like anyone. He was all alone. In his heyday, no one could touch him. He would make ten thousand dollars in a single week and be broke the next Monday. One year he had forty tailored suits and thirty pairs of shoes; the next year he lived in a boxcar in North Dakota. Bojangles Robinson was best man at his first marriage, and his friends included Wallace Beery, Billie Holliday, Jelly Roll Morton, Robert Mitchum, Dizzy Dean, Louis Armstrong, and Carmelo Batista. He had sung with Al Hibbler, boxed John Henry Lewis, danced with Bojangles, and made a movie with Robert Mitchum and Julie London. He knew and could imitate both Huey and Earl Long. He was also fisherman, cook, hunter, devoted family man, and born entertainer.

The man who called the *Star* came back and said the round was the twelfth. Then someone said, "How 'bout Billy Conn? How long he last?"

Satchel raised his voice. "Listen here, I saw that fight. Saw it in New York. Joe caught up with him in the thirteenth.

Caught him in the corner and drilled him. Hell, that wasn't no fight. Billy would peck at him like a sparrow and then run. Peck and run, peck and run, that's all he knew. He looked like a banty rooster worrying a bulldog. Joe put him clean away. That's when Joe came out with the saying, 'He can run, but he can't hide.' "

Satch was tall — six feet four — and lean, and hard. His eyes were clear, and when he smiled he looked twenty years younger than his sixty-odd years. Satch could imitate Casey Stengel, Phil Rizzuto, and Dizzy Dean, and when he did, he laughed so hard he had to stop talking. When he talked about his years with Cleveland and his conversations with Bill Veeck and Lou Boudreau, he took all three voices. We talked about fast cars, fights, catfish, carp, redbreast, barbecue, Southern politics, and moonshine, and finally — baseball.

"When I was pitching regular, I could thread a needle in the night. Used to practice control by pitching over a chewing-gum wrapper for home plate. And you talk about speed, why, those batters couldn't even see that ball at noon. Tell me something — if they can't see it, how they going to hit it?"

It was a good question, and as I sat there with him at the Twilight Zone Bowling Alley Bar and Grill trying to figure out how a man could be over sixty and look around forty and move as if he were thirty, I knew there were going to be a lot of unanswered questions about Leroy "Satchel" Paige.

The records show that in 1948, after Satchel had been pitching for more than twenty-five years in the Negro League and barnstorming around the country with his famous All Stars and the Kansas City Monarchs, he was signed to pitch for the Cleveland Indians, then owned by Bill Veeck. In his first start against the Chicago White Sox, he pitched before one of the strangest baseball crowds ever assembled. Comiskey Park in Chicago was jammed with

Paige fans. There were twelve thousand outside the park listening on radios. Inside the park were five to six thousand more *with tickets*, standing on ramps and in back aisles, unable to see or hear the game's progress. They could only shout questions and cheer when they heard Satchel had done something. And he did do something that first night in the majors: He shut out Chicago. Three days later, back in Cleveland, he shut them out again. The records of these games are no more astonishing than the records of Satch's whole career. In many books he is credited with two hundred and fifty shutouts and at least twenty-five no-hitters. He is reputed to have pitched doubleheaders and won both games, and it is pretty well established that he appeared in four to five thousand games. His favorite trick was to call in his entire outfield, and then strike out the side. But surpassing the records and the tricks of Satchel Paige was the sign posted on the parks where he and his All Stars appeared:

SATCHEL PAIGE * WORLD'S GREATEST PITCHER * GUARANTEED TO STRIKE OUT THE FIRST NINE MEN OR YOUR MONEY BACK.

Later at Satch's home, I asked him which batters gave him the most trouble.

He stretched back on the couch, shook his head and smiled. "Well, let's see now. When you get right down to it, I guess I got to say none of them gave me any *real* trouble. Now, I ain't saying they never hit back then — I'm not saying that at all. 'Cause we had us more good hitters than they got now, and you better believe that. Man, that crowd could *hit*. The one that *could* have given me the most trouble was old Josh — Josh Gibson. He's been dead a good while now. Oh, he was something to see. He was generally on my team, so we didn't play against each other too much, but I'm telling you who *could* have given me trouble. When Josh was playing, wasn't no one around could get a ball by him. Hell, if they wouldn't give him something good to hit at, he'd take something bad. Used to jump out and get it if it came anywhere near the plate. Josh hit 'em flat-footed, little like Ted Williams. But he was stronger than Ted. Lord, he was *strong*. Didn't have much legs, got his power from up in here." Satch drew a line across his chest. "But he had it there, no doubt about that. He was the best — the very best."

Rita Jean came back into the living room and said she wanted a dime for the ice-cream man. Satch gave her a dime and she ran out. "You take some cash customer back there paying four bits to see us play, well, I'll tell you something — that scutter really got his money's worth, and I want you to know it. 'Cause he ain't ever going to see baseball like that again. Nosir, not round here he ain't. Yeah Bo, them were times, them were tall times."

They must have been times. Nickel hot dogs, dime beer, and teams like the Homestead Grays, the Chattanooga Black Lookouts, the Birmingham Black Barons, the Mobile Tigers, Gus Greenlee's Pittsburgh Crawfords, and the famous Kansas City Monarchs. And the men — Poindexter Williams, Bullet Joe Rogan, Sweet Juice Johnson, Home Run Brown, Cool Papa Bell, Josh Gibson, and Satchel Paige. No, there won't be any more of those times around. These men lived baseball — lived it, ate it, slept it. They knew nothing else. When the season ended they barn-stormed, and when barnstorming ended in the winter, they headed for the tropics. They didn't own insurance agencies, bowling alleys, or bars. They didn't write advertising copy or endorse cereals or cigarettes for big money — all they knew was baseball. Satch said, "Oh, but they could *play*, pod-ner."

The Negro League of the 1930s and 1940s is gone now. With integration in the sports world opening the way for Negroes to play in the majors, and the gradual decline of baseball because of television and changing franchises, most of the Negro teams have disbanded. They left behind no records and only a few photographs. They had no Cooperstown.

In 1934 and 1935, Satch had an All Star team that beat Dizzy Dean's National League All Stars four games out of six. After the last of these games, Dean said that Paige was the greatest pitcher he had ever seen. He added, "If me and Satch had been together at St. Louis, we would have clenched the pennant by July and gone fishing from then till it was time to come back for the World Series."

Dean retired with an injury a few years later, and Bob Feller organized an All Star team composed from the American and National leagues. The Bob Feller All Star Team is still considered the best team ever fielded. Paige, with his regular infield of Gibson, Bell, Johnson, and Brown, beat Feller's All Stars five games out of eight, on the Pacific Coast. In the games against the Dean and Feller teams, Satchel is considered to have reached his pitching high-water mark. Thirteen years after this, he was admitted to the majors. Bob Feller once said, "The pre-war Paige was the best I ever saw, and I'm judging him on the way he overpowered or outwitted some of the best big-league hitters of the day."

Satchel pitched his first pro baseball back in 1922 for the Mobile Tigers. Twenty-six years later he made the majors, for in 1948 he was called up by the Cleveland Indians. In 1950 he went with the St. Louis Browns, and after they dropped his option, because of age, he returned to the Kansas City Monarchs in 1953 and played exhibition games around the country. In 1955 he played for Bill Veeck again, this time with the Miami Marlins of the International League. Satch was around fifty at that time, and even then he led the league, allowing only 1.5 earned runs per game. In 1957 with Miami he had a 2.42 average, and in 1961 in the Pacific Coast League, pitching for the Portland Beavers, he managed to hold it down to 2.88. For several years after that, Satch had his own All Stars. One month they are called the Harlem Stars, the next, the Satchel Paige All Stars. In the late sixties, he even served a season as a pitching coach with the Atlanta Braves.

He talked about pitching that first year in the majors. "Hell, when I got up to Cleveland I was pitching them the same way I did when I was with Mobile and Birmingham twenty-five years earlier. Slow and easy, that's the way I moved, but I had me my Stinger going and that ball would hop like there was a magnet in it.

"Old Boudreau like to had a fit when he saw how I could field bunts and throw to first while I was still bent over. I remember the first bunt I fielded against the Yankees — Boudreau commenced to shouting, 'Satch, ain't you got some better way to throw that ball? It's so late to be doing that [Cleveland was in a late-August pennant drive]. Looks like you going to throw that ball *clean* away.' And Bill Veeck had to come out of the dugout and calm him down, 'Boudreau, you leave that man alone. That man's been throwing that way for seventy years. What the hell we going to be teaching him now? We better just sit back and watch him.' "

I asked Satch what it was like against Chicago that first time.

He said, "What do you mean?"

I asked for some kind of comparison, and he shook his head as if he were disappointed in me. "Wasn't like anything. You can't compare it. I tell you what it was like, it was nice, real nice. I'll tell you something else. I wouldn't mind being around them boys right now. I still got my Stinger and I can still hold any team on earth three or four innings. But you just wait till the hot weather comes back. I'll be breaking out of here."

I asked him how often he pitched when he was barnstorming.

"Every day. And I mean, I don't get all that rest those boys get in the majors on those feather beds. When I go to bed it's generally right there in my station wagon. But I got to start facing it — I just ain't no spring chicken anymore. Hell, you take me when I was going strong. I'd pitch doubleheaders, then drive three or four hundred miles, sleep in the car, and get up with my glove in my hand and pitch another full game. And if you don't think that will work on you and tear you down after a while, you better back off. And that night ball will cut up your old butt, too. Gets too cold out there."

He began talking about the Yankees. "Now that Mickey Mantle, that's my boy. That boy could *move* when he first came up as a rookie. Hell, he could bat .400 just laying down bunts. Pitchers couldn't move fast enough for him and there ain't a third baseman alive that's fool enough to crowd in on him. First time he bunted on me, he batted left-handed. I sprang out toward the third base line and picked it up and whipped it over — hell, that man had already passed first and was cruising back, wiping the sweat off with his hat. Mickey was something, all right. Lord, as a rookie, there never was a man like him. I tell you what I think: If they hadn't been for those operations and all, he would have been the greatest of them all.

"I remember one time, I had me a little fun off him. He was a sucker for my hesitation pitch. I gave him a double windup one time and then hesitated at the top, and I'll be dogged if he didn't start his swing before the ball left my hand. Then when I let the ball go, he swung again and missed. I told the umpire he should call two strikes. But they wouldn't allow that. But you couldn't fool him too much, nosir. He caught on fast." Mantle said of Paige, "He was the best I ever faced in a pinch."

"I pitched against them Yankees many times. I gave them a crying fit up there, and I like to drove old Casey Stengel crazy. They'd generally shoot me in there along about the seventh inning and I'd clamp down on them hard. Old Casey would get up around the fifth inning and commence running up and down the dugout steps. He runs around there like a chicken you just spilt hot grease on, and he starts into shouting, 'All right, now, I wants me them runs now. We gots to have them runs now. Old Father Time (that's what he called me) is coming. He ain't got but one ball, but he ain't going to give you *nothing.*' "

Satchel pitched to Joe DiMaggio on the West Coast, before Joe went to the Yankees. According to Satchel (and the records), DiMaggio never gave Satchel much trouble. The scouts were watching Joe and one day after he played against Satchel, they wired to Yankee headquarters, "DiMaggio all we had hoped for; he hit Satch one for four."

In one game for Cleveland, when they were playing the Yankees, they brought Satchel in with the bases loaded and three balls and no strikes on the batter. Phil Rizzuto was on third, hitching up his pants and dancing around, getting set to come home. The legend has it that Satch walked by Rizzuto and said, "Don't you go getting nervous there, little fellow. You ain't going nowhere." He didn't. Satch retired the side.

"I like Ted Williams, too. Ted lost his best years in the service, but that was all right. I mean — you couldn't fool him, either. He hit 'em flat-footed, like Josh, and he had himself a pair of eyes that wouldn't quit. You remember how they all said Ted pulled everything to right field? Hell, Ted had that American League scared to death. Old Boudreau played him to the right, called it the Boudreau shift or the Williams shift or some fool thing. Well, I cured him of that. I'd put all them fielders in left field and then I'd make Ted hit to left. I proved that Ted wasn't no pull hitter.

You pitch a left-handed man low and outside and how's he going to pull to right? Can't be done. You bring them up around the letters, and *shame on you*. Ted gets it and it's going four miles like a bullet. Hell, a man's a fool to pitch Ted any way but low and outside. That's where you got to have that fine control going. I had me that control then — and I still got it."

That evening Satch took me to Gates Place for what he told me was the best barbecue in the country. Everyone at Gates knew him, and they all came over and shook his hand. "You won't find better barbecue in the whole United States of America. Hell, them cooks up North throw some kind of mess at you and they call it barbecue sauce. Most time it's mustard with some vinegar and hot sauce, and I don't know what all. Listen, when you get back East, you tell them about Gates."

I asked him about the story that he never ate anything fried.

"That's them reporters. Let me ask you something. How am I going to cook eggs in the morning when I'm out on the road? And what about bacon and ham and sausage? What am I going to do with that? Here I am on some gravel road four hundred miles from nowhere, what kind of breakfast am I going to cook on my Coleman if I can't fry something? Maybe they figure I eat cornflakes? Yeah, yeah, that would do it. Yeah, a nice bowl of cornflakes, maybe put me on some berries, some strawberries would be nice, and a little milk. Yeah, like they show in the advertisements. Oh, that would be real nice. Then I climb back in that wagon, and I drive four hundred more miles to the next town. And when I stop, I got to get out with my glove in my hand 'cause I got to start throwing. Yeah, them cornflakes would do it up just about right. Maybe they figure I stop along the road and get me a couple slices of bologna and some light bread.

"You got to be strong to follow the roads I follow and put

out the kind of day I put out. How many men my age you
know could drive four hundred miles after sleeping in the
car and then hop out and start throwing fast balls?

"Hell, you talk to them fool reporters and they write
anything. And every dern one of them copies the next. I
read the same story about me not eating fried foods forty
times, and there ain't a lick of it true."

Satch said he was beginning to pace himself, and that he'd
like to live back down South where he could fish all year and
raise his own vegetables. "I'm what you call a fish demon. I
took Lahoma down South a while back and I mean, we
fished almost every day. She just loved it. Got plenty of
shrimps and prawns and crabs, plenty of bream and bass
and redbreasts — ain't no better eating fish in the world
than that redbreast, nosir. I tell you something else and you
can mark this down as a prediction. You give this country
twenty or thirty more years, and everybody's got any sense
is going down South. Now you take it down there in the
Carolinas, and over to Louisiana and then down into
Florida. Why, it's like a garden. That's where a man can live.
Hell, you want to get yourself some fish, you just walk out
your back door and stick your pole in the river and you got
them. That's when they're good — fresh like that. Then say
you want yourself some fresh vegetables — I don't mean
none of this frozen mess they throwing at you nowadays. I
said fresh vegetables. Like you want yourself some collards
— you just go out in the backyard and just reach down and
get them. 'Cause they right there. Then say you want some
turnips or some rutabeggers with them collards, why you
just reach down and scratch around and you get them, too.
And maybe you got a bean vine whipping around the porch
to keep the dogs cool. Why, you jut reach out and pick them
right there.

"Course, you got to know what you're doing down there.
You just can't go reaching under just any old rock. They got

a few snakes down there. You take your moccasin, what you call him? Yeah, your cottonmouth, now he's *bad*. When he chomps down on you, you got yourself some trouble. I've seem them so thick swimming along they stuck up like fingers — looked like they were going to invade some place.

"Then they got a turtle down there, called the Blue. He's mean, too. You go sticking your fingers near him and you ain't coming back with nothing. Nosir, he takes it all. I used to hang over them little bridges near the Everglades and look down in the water. Man, you look down there and see some of those *operations* cruising by and they send shivers down you."

Satch ordered barbecued lamb with no sauce. I ordered mine with plenty of sauce. When we finished there wasn't enough meat for a cat. I asked him if he had any regrets.

"Naw, I ain't got none that I make a fuss about. I had me a few disappointments, but we all have a lot of them. Oh, I figure I should have been called up to the majors long before they sent for me. I was pushing forty-five when I went up with Cleveland, and I would like to have shown the folks what I could do when I was thirty or so. But I didn't let them down. I threw me some good ball then, and I'm still throwing it. But I had me all that good juice going when I was in my thirties; I had me so much energy, I didn't know what to do with it."

When Jackie Robinson, the first Negro to play in the majors, was called up to Brooklyn in 1945, Satch was not only disappointed — he was angry. Everyone had told him he was certain to be the first choice. It is said that when Lahoma asked Satch whom the majors had called, Satch said, "That kid on second base. I forget his name."

"Lot of times I go into the dressing room with a headache on account of all the money troubles I got myself in. Never could hold on to that green. That stuff goes like it has wings. But the minute I get me my uniform on and my socks and shoes fixed, that headache is gone. Then the minute I take off that uniform, here she comes back. Like I said, you love something the way I love baseball and ain't nothing going to bother you when you playing. And that's the way it's been with me all my life."

The Frog Jump

D EAR JOE, I can't believe you're coming down. And without the little woman. How'd you manage that? Speaking of little women, mine isn't so little, so don't be mentioning Detroit. I'd hate taking a Q and A on what all we were doing up there.

Now listen, once you cross that Tennessee line, you are officially in the South, so slow down. Friend, they've got radar traps that fire off when they just see that license plate. They figure anyone from Cook County, Illinois, is either transporting controlled substances or running from the federals, so they just scoop up all of you and then sort out the innocent in the morning. So be sure and bring along your driver's license, birth certificate, car registration, and several recent photographs, and anything you can think of that proves the car is yours and paid for and that you are native born. If you're carrying guns or grenades or heavy ammo, they'll leave you alone. But don't be trying to sneak any whiskey or beer or wine by them. In the event you're nailed, switch your radio over to a PTL station and pretend you were caught up in a Chuck Colson message and got excited and squeezed down on the gas. If you can't handle that, take my advice and keep absolutely quiet. The minute those rednecks hear you pronouncing every letter in every word and ringing those g's, they'll think you're a member of the Red Menace, handcuff you to the steering wheel, and tow you in.

Now, I know you claim you don't like bluegrass music. Problem is, you've just been hearing it in the wrong places. When you get on some old Tennessee or Georgia back road, with the mules and the cotton and the "R U Ready for Eternity" painted on automobile tires and nailed to the fence posts, and the dogs all standing around in threes and fours, I guarantee it's going to make a difference. You take the same music and hear it in a Lakeshore traffic jam, and it will give you a four-day migraine.

Listen, Memphis is a mess, but if you've got to see Graceland, go on out and get it over with. They've got a twenty-foot bronze statue of Elvis out there that people are holding crippled children up to. He looks too much like Prince Valiant to suit me; you look in his eyes real close. I mean, *no one* can look that sincere. It's like he's looking out over the Dead Sea and he's thinking about a new way to travel.

From Memphis, cut over to Chattanooga and then drop straight on down to Atlanta. As you come South, you will notice the pace definitely slowing down; the air will sweeten, and you will see flowers and fauna, unfamiliar to your jaded eyes, that cannot survive in the harsh latitudes you are leaving behind. Just kidding, sport, but no lie, the average Yankee knows about as much about the South as a hog knows about the Lord's plan for salvation. Of course, people down here get a warped idea of what Chicago and New York are like, too. Uncle Martin Luther said he was riding on the New York Central train through "a place

called the Bronx" and he saw a man holding a little
fox-terrier-type dog out of a sixth-story window to relieve
himself. Martin came back and laughed about that for six or
seven years. Kept saying, "Lord, I just don't know how folks
can live like that." And Aunt Bess, that's his wife, would pat
his knee and say, "Well, hon, it just goes to show that it takes
all kinds of people to make a world."

Speaking of New York, you can talk about going out to
see that little zoo out on Staten Island and that boat trip we
took around Manhattan, but listen, don't go mentioning
anything else. Maude can pick up on just anything.

Now, Joe, when you get hungry, don't go eating in those
interstate chains. You get off that road and get back on the
mixed tar and gravels and find you an old-fashioned diner.
Get back in there where they read heads and work roots and
fry hamburgers and pork chops and ain't afraid of a little
grease. Grease, old buddy, that's the secret of the South.

And speaking of grease, you are in for what some people
call a "gastronomical cornucopia," because I'm getting an
overnight pass and you and me are going to the Springfield
Frog Jump, and they serve a barbecue there that will knock
you down.

O.K., a few words about barbecue. First of all, when you
arrive in the Palmetto State, you are in the official Tigris
and Euphrates land of barbecue. I mean, right down in
here is where it all began. Check it out: the Garden of Eden
of Barbecue, Thessalonians 6 and 7. Now I know you've
heard how Texas claims they have the best. Well, I shall now
put that myth to rest. The Lone Star State, while they may
have many things, does not have hickory wood. Without
hickory wood you cannot have barbecue. Now they may call
it barbecue, because it's a free country and they can call
anything they cook and serve and eat anything they want.
But around here, if you mention Texas barbecue,
someone's going to drift out to the parking lot and check

your license plates. Down here in the hard-lard belt, barbecue is cooked with hickory wood and the sauce is either mustard based or vinegar-and-pepper based. And that, friend, is the long and the short of it. Now North Carolina has hickory wood and they have on occasion been known to produce a good cross-breed hog. But your basic North Carolinian does not have good sense, because they will drench down that pork with catsup-based sauce and that will not do it.

As far as I'm concerned — and friend, I have been a barbecue judge on more than one occasion and I do not treat it lightly — I will not even discuss catsup-based sauce. But South Carolina barbecue will cross that finish line as tender as pound cake, and with our sauces and light bread and cole slaw and cold beer, it will drop you to your knees, where you will weep tears of appreciation and never-ending gratitude. At the Springfield Frog Jump, I have seen serious men in business suits and full-grown women go into what is called a "barbecue coma."

But the barbecue and the beer is only the beginning of things down here in Springfield. The big move, and why they come from seventeen states away, is the jumping of the frogs. Alex, this buddy of mine, and I came down last year, and it was a pure and unadulterated mess. We left Columbia around noon with a case of Bud, so by the time we got there we were absolutely not responsible for anything. First thing we did was buy two bullfrogs from this kid who swore he had raised them on an all-protein and Vitamin C diet and they were guaranteed to soar. This is how it works. You put your frog on a starting pad. Then when the referee drops the flag, you turn him loose. He jumps three times and the judge measures the total distance. Record down here in the swamp is seventeen feet six inches. The world's record — nineteen feet two inches — is out at the Super Bowl of Frog Jumping in Calavaras County, California.

The winner here (the frog and the owner) gets a free trip to Calavaras on the governor's jet plane to compete in the nationals. Anyhow, here we are trying to keep out of the one hundred and ten-degree heat with these frogs in a covered box, with ice chips to keep them cool and ferns to make them feel at home, waiting for the starting time. Us and about four thousand rednecks. Well, we lurch around the town of Springfield for a couple of hours, and all there is to do is look at the snake show and drink Budweiser and eat barbecue — which we did, brother, which we did. Well, the time finally comes, and we get up on stage with the politicians, who are all running for office or they wouldn't be here in all this heat and aggravation, and the chiropractors who have recently been declared legal, and a couple of enterprising acupuncturists. Finally, Alex and I have to step forward and announce our frogs' names. Well, we've come up with Ethel and Julius Rosenberg. Tasteless, right? Well, no one laughed, and no one booed, or no one did anything, because no one had ever heard of them, which includes the politicians (which will give you some idea of the literary habits of the leaders of the great Palmetto State). Well, Alex and I get our frogs ready at the starting pad. Now, what Alex has done is, he's talked the snake show owner into lending us a five-foot-long black snake (non-lethal), and he has him in a paper sack. The method of operation was very simple. When the frog was on the pad and ready to be launched, Alex would suddenly introduce the snake. Since a snake is supposed to scare hell out of a frog, we figured the frog would leap out of there like Evel Knievel into an eighteen-foot South Carolina record, and we'd be on the governor's jet plane to California in the morning.

O.K., so I'm squatting down there holding Julius by his hips and shoulder blades, and I signal ready. The judge drops his checkered flag, and Alex makes his move with the paper bag and the black snake. Well, the frog takes one long, hard look at him. Then he puffs up and starts panting. Then he relieves himself all over my hands. Then he jumps about a foot straight up and about two inches out, and there he freezes, staring at the snake and waiting for Armageddon. Needless to say, you did not get any funny postcards from Calavaras County, California.

You know, old buddy, I'm not your basic Paul Harvey type, who always tries to make things make sense, but a lot of the great Southland has to be seen to be appreciated. I mean, there's got to be some reason why we put up with all this hookworm and low per capita income and poor crops and general abuse. But I'll tell you one thing we've solid got down here — the sun. We've got more sun than we can handle. If it wasn't for air conditioning and Coca-Cola, we'd be shut down from twelve to three every day, the way they do it down in old Mexico. On the other hand, Martin Luther always says there's a lot less insanity in Georgia and South Carolina than there is up in Big Ten Country. Said the reason is, you people have cloud-cover three and four months a year, and when a man can't see his shadow for that long, his timing gear starts slipping, and he starts needing some front end work. And I'll tell you something else we have down here — funerals. No lie, old-fashioned screaming, and praying, and singing, and falling-down-in-the-dirt funerals.

Up in Chicago and New York, if somebody dies, it's a state secret. Down here, it's just another excuse to bring over a covered dish and get together and hear some music out under the pecans. I hit one a few months back and old Aunt Bess said, "Lord, child, you should have been here last year. We were burying them like hogs. I bet I put up fourteen hams and I don't know how many pecans pies and gallons of cole slaw." And then again, if some loony has an advanced case of "Dungeons and Dragons" and decides to slow it down with, say a twelve-gauge or two heaping tablespoons of strychnine, the papers report the suicide as "after a short illness." Up there, the *Daily News and Mirror* will show you the body and poison and the priest comforting the weeping widow and the wailing kids. What I'm saying is — we have a sense of propriety down here.

And speaking of propriety, let's not be mentioning Phoenix or that place next door with all the Mexicans. Tiempo? Tempe? Quick story before I forget: The sheriff in the next county went on TV news last summer announcing he'd broke up this massage parlor ring out at the No-Tel Motel, and that he had in his possession fifty-six calling cards from prominent businessmen, faculty, chiropractors, and highly-placed clergymen. Said the next day at noon he was going to read the names in alphabetical order.Well, buddy, the phones started ringing. "George, you've got to get me off that damn list." "George, somebody stole my cards. I was in Atlanta all last month." "George, please. Please take care of me." And some old Republican came in with "George, for God's sake, *put me on* that list and read it out loud and clear. Then you can take me to the polls in November and just point me at that Democratic lever."

This thing is getting too long. I better close now before Maude comes in and wants to read it. Listen, when you hit the first exit on I-77, bear right and keep right until you see a Ramada Inn. It will read "Hey Joe!" (that's you), then it will say "Don't Mention Drake Hotel" (that'll be me). We're near here on a road with no name, so pull off and call me and I'll come out and get you. Man, that first beer with you is going to taste nice.

Discreetly Yours,
Billy

The Late, Great
Medicine Show

B ACK BEFORE World War II, when ground chuck was moving at twenty-one cents a pound and bacon fifteen, a dollar bill bought a four-ounce bottle of miracle tonic water and two full hours of one of the world's greatest medicine shows. Promoters and impresarios would announce a cast of star acts that would make Vegas producers jealous, and the medicine they hawked was billed to cure everything from nervous prostration to "the big knee." There were big shows, great shows: Silas Green from New Orleans; Rabbit Foot out of Vicksburg, Mississippi; Snookum Nelson and his Creole Brothers; and Doc Bartok's Bardex Minstrels. A typical show packed in four thousand under the big tent while another two thousand stood looking through the open side walls as Bessie Smith and Bojangles Robinson would belt out the new songs and do the new wild dances. They were big acts, bright and brassy acts. And the bands backing them up, dressed in flashy satin tuxedos with matching top hats and checkered vests, have left sounds out under the pecan trees and the chinaberries that are still there.

The big touring groups crossed the country like comets throwing off sparks and setting fires in the dry timber. But, like comets, they burned out when the government outlawed freewheeling medicine sales in the early fifties. Some of the stars moved into radio, television, and the movies, but many acts without the medicine money went into winter quarters near Sarasota, Florida, and have been there ever since.

Doc Milton Bartok — creator of Bardex Tonic, Bardex Minstrels — and Walking Mary Smith told me about it. Walking Mary, the sister of Bessie Smith, was dressed in a flowing, flowery muumuu with a matching purse and headband and plastic fruit-basket earrings. She wore diamonds in her teeth. "We had us stars back in then. Stars! Nowdays all a person's got to do is scream a couple licks, and he's got his own special on television. . . . I just don't know what happened to people's taste."

Doc aimed a pistol finger at her. "My secret was always keeping everything local and dealing with people right there on their own level."

Every year for more than twenty years, Doc and the Bardex Minstrels — with their comics, singers, dancers, musicians, and a carload of Bardex — left Florida in April and followed the strawberry, bean, tomato, and peanut crops north. They played every night except Sunday, and by August they would be deep in the Pennsylvania hill country. Here, they turned around and headed back to get the tobacco workers and the cotton pickers in the Carolinas and Georgia before the rain and the cold weather set in. Doc and Mary talked about the comics they had known and worked with. After listing Nipsey Russell, Red Skelton, Mickey Rooney, Stepin Fetchit (originally two men, one Stephan, one Fetchet), and Redd Foxx, they agreed that the best was "Sparky" Anderson out of Albany, Georgia. Doc shook his head. "We had to have special heavyduty seats when he was on. People would tear up regular seats. They'd rare back and jump up and walk around and laugh so hard they'd wind up hugging one another."

Mary told how wild and original Sparky was and how even Bojangles himself learned something from him. They talked about the Bally Wagons, where the entire band rode into town stacked up fifteen feet in the air on top of a horse-drawn wagon, while the local kids and the noon drunks would dance in the streets. Of the crazy acts where a woman would drag a man down the street with a rope tied around his neck to attract a crowd. And they talked about the death of Bessie Smith outside Lulu, Mississippi.

In the thirties and forties, the movie houses couldn't compete with the free medicine shows, and many simply closed their doors until the show rolled on into the next town. Mary remembered it all. "We'd be playing a town of maybe two hundred, and along about first dark here, they'd come. They'd be coming down the railroad tracks carrying their shoes tied around their necks. The parents would be on the paths, but the kids were on the rails. And they'd be bringing us iced tea and fresh flowers and pies and cakes. And if we were near an apron factory or an overalls mill, they'd be bringing some of that, too. I tell you we were *all* they had. They treated us like *kings and queens*."

Doc met his wife Betty at the Detroit fairground when he was pitching medicine from the rumble seat of his Terraplane. Her father, Doctor Jacobs, had his own medicine show, with her mother billed as Irene the Girl With the X-Ray Eyes. It was a medicine show romance. Doc asked Betty, who was then sixteen, where their next show date was. Betty, in true show biz fashion, told him the opposite direction. It was this that won the heart of Doc Milton Bartok, and he and Betty were together from then on. Betty, who was exactly half of the act when Doc was pitching, would move around in the crowd feeling out the audience and deciding when Doc should stop the pitch and start making the sales.

Doc talked about pitching. "It's always a good idea to keep your crowd on its feet. A man sitting down has a tough time getting at his wallet. You want him ready when you're ready."

He told how Billy Graham sold Fuller Brushes back in North Carolina, and how he used the tried-and-true hypnotic pendulum technique of moving back and forth and side to side. Less sophisticated then, "the pendulum" is the hard sell "peeler pitch," named from selling potato peelers at dime and novelty stores. "Ed McMahon was and still is one of the best in the business. You watch his next dog food commercial."

Doc worked the medicine show route for twenty years and then, attracted by the elephants, the cat acts, the midway, and the high wire, he bought out Hunt Brothers, changed the name to Bartok's Famous Circus, and was back on the road again. With seven elephants, cast of two hundred, and twenty-nine trucks, Doc became one of the best front men in the business. The front man, a vanishing breed on the American scene, goes into a town, visits the restaurants, the stores, checks the prices, the accents, and finds out where the allegiances are and the power is. With this information, he can decide whether the show should be rural, redneck, black, mixed, segregated, sophisticated, blue collar, or what. "You name it, we had the book on it. Then up in Pennsylvania, you got your Amish and your Mennonites. They'd come in droves in their little black buggies and bonnets, and they solid loved a good show. But it had to be clean. No dirt, none."

Doc said that with the decline of the circus, most of the famous front men had joined the political machines. As advance men they are worth their weight in gold.

Doc and Mary talked about the nights and the roads, the

lights and the towns. Of truck tractors doubling back one hundred miles four and five times a night to pick up the big trailers; of triple turns, where an aerialist in the first act would be on the teeterboard in the second, and selling snow cones in the third. Of Nubian lions and Bengal cats, white rhinos and plastic whales. And of the dynamite-lettered big shows that unload at dawn at the railroad yards and brass-spangled elephant parades into small towns that will never see their like again. They talked about the legendary Wendy Van Hooten Circus fairy tale told to the circus kids. How the red-white-and-blue, expanding-rubber big top could seat five hundred or five thousand or fifty thousand and could be floated from one town to the next by giant, colored balloons. Of the glass center king poles with goldfish swimming inside, and brass quarter poles, and stakes that gleamed in a sun that always shone when Wendy Van Hooten came to town. They told about the superstitions. How an ax blade laid across the wind would cut the deadly gales in half and save the big tents. And of the mojos from the Seven Sisters of Algiers that guaranteed good luck in love, gambling, and moonshining and counteracted the devil's graveyard dust sprinkled by Doctor Death himself on his nightly rounds.

Doc spread photographs and souvenirs out on the coffee table, and he and Mary pointed out old and dead friends. Some were rehearsing in the backyard, others were clowning around the cook house, and one long, narrow shot framed in mica-flecked cardboard showed a group at a 1930 pitchman's convention at Atlantic City. But one old curled and yellowed photograph, of a medicine troop at a railroad platform posing stylishly before their trunks of costumes and medicine, caught it all. The women were wearing high-collared long dresses, fur muffs, and veiled hats. The men, looking pleased with themselves, were holding big cigars at sophisticated angles. Somehow, standing there in the slanting sun in front of the long-gone City of New Orleans, the cameraman had caught that fragile mixture of sly cunning and innocence reserved for little kids selling Chiclets and their sisters. Doc smiled, fingering the grained and faded print. "They were simpler times back then. Simpler. People hadn't been so exposed and they trusted everyone. Even strangers."

The afternoon sun that had balanced on the edge of Sarasota Bay had finally set, and in the distance the neon along the coast highway was reflecting in the low clouds. Doc said when Betty was in the hospital the previous year, Mary would call her every day and sing her all the old songs. He asked her to sing again. Mary closed her eyes and, rocking slightly, slid into a soft, liquid "Sweet Georgia Brown." With no backup, no pitch pipe, nothing but her own tone-true voice, she swayed for rhythm and worked her long fine fingers in slow pulls and easy snaps and brought it all back. Then she sang "That Lonesome Road" and then her own song, "The Walking Blues."

Mary stood up to leave, and bowing her head she prayed for everyone's health. Then she prayed for world peace and the everlasting life. And finally she squeezed her hands together, and asked that her dearest friends, the Bartoks, would get the old group together soon and take her out on the road just one more time.

Mary was gone, and Doc sorted through the photographs, making a stack of the acts and stars that were still around. "Here's Clarence, my drummer. He can get me a band. And that's Buck Able. If he can't come up with four or five comics, hell ain't hot. And you heard Mary sing. All I need is a tent, and you know what I'm going to do?"

He answered his own question. "I'm going to make some bookings. By God, I'll show them what entertainment is. I bet this new generation would go crazy seeing an old-time medicine show."

Spaghetti
Western

OUT OVER THE north Atlantic, peeling back the Pan American cellophane from the Pan American knife, the Pan American fork, and the Pan American spoon, I thought about my assignment for *The Saturday Evening Post*. I was to meet producer Guido Di Renzo in Rome and go with him to the mountains of Yugoslavia and cover the filming of a cast-of-thousands Italian western. Visions of a good, fast, funny story. Vino instead of red-eye. Spaghetti and meatballs instead of jerky and beans. *"Va bene straniero, come ti chiamano?"* instead of "All right, stranger, what do they call you?"

As I sliced the chicken Kiev and salted it down, I saw myself in a Serbo-Croatian restaurant set against the Transylvanian Alps. I was asking for their native dish, their local wine, while my guide — a heavy and hairy Akim Tamiroff — was shouting for more gypsies, more violins.

Checked into Hotel d'Inghilterra in downtown Rome and, after tipping the operator ten dollars, asked her to locate Guido Di Renzo. Upstairs, in the same room where

Lord Byron shaved and slept and brushed his curly locks, I propped up my feet on the terrace rail and began sipping the house brandy. The terrace overlooks the rose roofs, the chimney pots, and the sun that set on the Caesars, the Gracchis, the Augustans. Two blocks over is the Via Corso, where Nero had his chariot races. At the height of his career, he thought he was a charioteer, an actor, a musician, an astrologist, and a lover. Drivers who raced him would resort to falling out, getting their feet tangled in the spokes, and smacking into the walls to make sure they lost. Any driver who beat Nero usually wound up talking it over with the lions on Saturday.

An hour later, when I came downstairs to see the sights, the operator said she was having trouble locating Di Renzo, but she would keep on trying.

I rented a German-built Ford called a Taunus. Nice riding car, but heavy as a tank and too wide for Roman streets. Funny how the roads vary; at a piazza (where four and five roads come together and six coffee houses compete) you could take a sixteen-wheel semi-rig and make a three hundred and sixty degree turn with no strain. One block later, you hit a paved footpath called an avenue that you couldn't skin a wheelbarrow down. Then, of course, every block has a different name. At home, Main Street is Main Street until it hits the Broad River Road. Over here, a street can have ten Italian-general names in ten blocks — which makes road map reading not a casual thing. I spotted an American Express tour bus and whipped in behind to follow it. First stop was the Sistine Chapel. I parked the Taunus and got in line with a group of tourists from Mississippi and Alabama. Couple in front were from Mobile. He had on bermudas, Hush Puppies, and a purple, transparent shirt with six camera and light meter straps cutting across him like a Mexican ammunition bearer. His wife, with a buzz-saw-cutting-through-green-pine voice, announced to everyone, "We saw *The Agony and the Ecstasy* six times, getting ready for this experience." She emphasized "experience." Her husband, her biggest supporter, pointed up into the dome. "Imagine having a piece of talent like that and having to suffer the way he did. I just can't feature it. Listen, if y'all ain't seen Charlton Heston playing Michelangelo, all I'm saying is you're missing one of the all-time great performances."

The Sistine Chapel was enough sightseeing, so I picked up the Appian Way, then the Via Corso, and tooled the big Taunus back to check on Mr. Guido Di Renzo. Bad news at the hotel. No Guido Di Renzo. The operator suggested we try Di Renzo Guido. In a few minutes, she called back saying no one had heard of either name, and I began wondering if I could do an article on the cathedrals of Rome.

In the morning there was a cable from *The Post:* "Di Renzo deal in Yugoslavia off temporarily. Find another western and proceed with story." I told the operator and the concierge my problem. After five phone calls, they announced they had not only found a western, they had found a producer. I was to meet Sylvester Santini at the Café Doney on the Veneto in fifteen minutes.

To the Roman moviemaker, director, actor, and script writer, the Veneto is the absolute center of the world. Unlike the Sunset Strip, where the hot-rodders can drag the half-mile stretch from Schwab's Drug Store all the way to the International House of Pancakes with no tight turns, the Veneto winds and dips through the hills of Rome like a thirsty snake looking for water. Facing each other across eight lanes of bumper-to-bumper Fiats are the two most popular sidewalk cafes in Rome, the Café de Paris and the Doney. Seated at an end table at the Doney with a carafe of white wine, a Cinzano ashtray, and wearing sunglasses as big as playing cards and as dark as sin, sat the producer Sylvester Santini.

When we shook hands and he told me to call him Santini, I knew it was going to be trouble. As a producer of independent films, he claimed he was the only person in town who could help me on my article. He pointed at a tall beard wearing his coat like a cape. "See him? Looks like a millionaire, doesn't he? Doesn't have a dime. He stole that suit and coat from Mastrionni's wardrobe five years ago." He laughed once. "Hell, check the names on the marquees. Look-alikes. Promoters think some sap will read Warren Beatton and pay his money, thinking it's Warren Beatty. One guy is trying out Clark Grant. Let me give you some warning, over here *they* will try out anything."

I asked him to tell me about his western.

Quickly he rubbed his hands together. "You'll love it. Love it."

Around us, big deals were as thick as flying ants around a beer sign. No one was discussing anything small. Hundred thousand dollar scripts, two hundred thousand dollar; four million dollar budgets, five, six. One deep, official-sounding voice under a Caligula haircut and glasses bigger and darker than Santini's said, "O.K., so we can't get Paul Newman. I say forget him. I personally know Robert Redford will *kill* for the part."

Santini whispered, "Now, there's something you've got to write about. Look." He hitch-hiked his finger at a table of ex-gladiators from the old muscle pictures behind us. Their biceps were bunched and straining out of their ripped-off sleeves. "Few years back, anyone with a set of pectorals and a fifty-inch chest was a star. Now they're dead. You put two guns and a holster on one of those guys, and he photographs like a locomotive."

I saw an opening and asked him what his budget was. He started to take off his glasses, then he changed his mind. "Five million. Five million, give or take a couple hundred thou. You've got to see the script. Sidney Lumet might, I'm

saying *might*, be my director. I got a call last night and they
say he loves it. Loves it."

I pulled out my pad and clicked my ballpoint down.

He reached over and closed my pad. "Look, chief, we can
do each other a lot of good. I can get you the hottest stories
in Rome. The hottest, got me? All I want in return is some
publicity for my property."

"Fair enough."

"O.K., let's put it on the table. We're not exactly shooting
a western, western. But it's close. Damn close. It's — well, it's
a Crusade movie. Twelfth century. Five million dollars
worth of horses, trick riding, sex, burning arrows, torture
scenes, mutilations, everything."

"A Crusade movie? You mean like *Richard the Lion-
Hearted*?"

Santini took off his glasses and leaned in close. He
needed some sleep. "It's the same as a western. Hell, most
movies are westerns anyway: good guys, bad guys, horses,
women. So they trade the horses for cards, or planes, or
German tanks, they're still the same as westerns. Basically,
it's the same old plot, the same old chase and explosions.
The only thing different is we have infidels instead of
Indians. If we put loin cloths on them and gave them
tomahawks, you wouldn't know the difference. Besides," he
laughed two notes, "it's tough for an Italian to look like an
Indian. Infidels, no problem."

Before I could say no, he was pointing me at a Charles
Manson-type with a Napoleonic hat, a full-length World
War I trench coat, and laced-up canvas leggings. "We call
him the Generalissimo. Watch."

The general paraded up and down in front of the Doney,
surveying the Café de Paris directly across the street. Then
he stopped, drew himself up to attention, and began
shouting out orders. "He thinks he's in charge of a battery
of cannons. Watch now, he's giving them the range. Now

the trajectory." Santini translated, "Ready on the right. . . .
Ready on the left. . . . Commence firing!"

The Generalissimo paused for a full minute, as the
phantom smoke blew away and he examined the carnage.
He bellowed out, *"Distrutto!"* Then he clicked his heels
together, saluted his fallen comrades, and marched off
down the Veneto.

Santini laughed. "Tomorrow, he'll be out in front of the
Café de Paris, and he'll destroy us. Same time, different
station."

Santini kept selling me on the Crusade-western idea, and
I went from no to maybe and finally that I'd have to think
about it. Later, I cabled *The Post* about the comic
possibilities, i.e., "Shootout at Jerusalem," "Crossbows and
Guitars," "How the East Was Won." *Post* answered quickly:
"Quit clowning around. Find a western and proceed as per
contract."

After another day of dodging Santini and still no luck,
the operator suggested that I simply drive out to Cinecitta,
the big movie center, and ask around. It sounded too easy,
but it made sense, and I drove out.

I pulled up to the Cinecitta gate looking for someone —
anyone — who knew anything. Crouching in over my
Getting-Along-in-Italian handbook, I asked the guard, who
spoke no English, if a western was being shot. He called
over a friend, who was more expressive with hands, more
expansive, more enthusiastic. He knew even less English,
but he was excited and kept saying that something very big
was going on inside. I said, "A western?" "Si." "You sure? A
western?" "Si, a western. . . . Si, si, si."

He led me through a series of doors toward a terrible
noise that seemed to be shaking everything. Finally, we
entered a block-long sound stage. I could hear hammering
and grinding at the far end and men shouting. He grabbed
my arms, squeezing and grinning. "A western!" It was the

only English word he seemed to know. We came around a high wall, and right in the middle of what I later learned was the world's largest construction shop, was a fifty-foot-high clipper ship with all sails flying. The foreman, a friend of my guide, climbed down and embraced us both. My guide, who had now transformed himself into my interpreter, told him that I was a journalist, and I was here to see the clipper ship. Both were talking and waving their arms at the same time. I think they were telling me how long they had worked on it, how proud they were, and how grateful they were that I was here. I finally said yes to everything, and that I would write nice things about them, and the ship, for indeed it was a wonderful ship. Back outside in the blazing sun, I pretended I was drawing two guns from a holster and made a bang-bang sound. My guide grinned and drew two more and fired off four rounds. I moved in close. "Where? Where is the bang-bang movie?" His smile vanished as he holstered his guns and shook his head.

Back at the hotel, Roman press headquarters had called and left word there was a Norwegian producer in town with a western, and I made the calls and set up the appointment. The producer's name was Swen and, like the ads for six hundred dollar sweaters, he looked like your basic ski instructor. While I didn't trust Santini from the minute I met him, I did like him. With Swen I didn't trust him or like him.

On the Veneto, when a girl passed, he would kiss his thumb and then, just loud enough and oily enough, he would whisper "*magnifico*." He said he had a western and they were already shooting, but he would tell me more later. First, we had to have drinks. Then came dinner. Normally, he said, he paid for everything, but since I was working for *The Post*, he knew I had to have receipts. In the days to come, he would more than make it up. Finally, in the corner

of a disco club and after two bottles of champagne, he told
me his plans. While he had the western script, the western
cast, and the western director, he needed some western (or
eastern) money. But, and here he winked, it was only a
matter of one more night. He let the bait trail and I bit.
"Night?" And then he closed in. He had a small ninety-five
horsepower plane that was almost silent. At night we
(suddenly it was *we*) would fly north to the great plains of
Italy and the home of the legendary Roman mounds. In the
moonlight, we would be able to see them outlined against
the sky. There we would silently land. And there we would
silently climb the mounds. And there, backlighted by the
full moon and the shimmering plain, with a Roto-Rooter
(he said he had the only one in Italy) we would drill down
through the top until we struck metal or ceramic. We would
open the mounds and remove the pots and pans and the
silver and the gold, and whatever the Romans and the
Etruscans had left behind. If I invested a mere two
thousand dollars — which would cover the plane expenses
and incidentals — I would net back fifty to seventy-five
thousand dollars, tax free, and ten percent of the western.
His eyes seemed bluer and smaller, and he seemed to be
weaving back and forth like a giant cobra, luring me in
closer, closer. For a minute I believed him. I think I was
saying "maybe" or "that's interesting" or "seventy-five
thousand." But then I noticed a girl had pressed herself
against the table and was asking if either of us would dance
with her. Swen brushed her away, as he kept his eyes on
mine. Suddenly, I shook my head and broke the spell and
leaped up with her. After leading her to the far end of the
floor, we danced out the whole set. Later, when we
returned to the table, there snugged under the Cinzano
ashtray with the bill, was Swen's card and CALL ME!

The next day, over expresso at the Café de Paris,
watching the Generalissimo inspect his Café Doney

battlements, Santini made me an offer I could not refuse. For four or five lines about him and his movie, he would guarantee he would deliver me to a western. I asked him if I could mention his trying to hustle me with the Crusade-western idea and make it humorous. He winced at the word "hustle" but recovered quickly. "That'll be O.K. My friends will love it. Main thing is be sure and spell the name right. And don't forget the movie, *The Cross and the Sword.*"

Santini called for a telephone and in less than an hour, in a chauffeur-driven, black Cadillac, we eased through the main gate at Cinecitta. We passed the rain-streaked and faded Corinthian columns from the Cleopatra filming days; we passed a German tank sitting low in the tall weeds outside a mock-up of Buchenwald, through a Swiss village, a New York street scene, a scale model of the Vatican, and an African village. Finally at the end of a rutted dirt street, complete with saloon, church, general store, blacksmith's shop, and sheriff's office, were lights, reflectors, cameras, a group of actors, horses, a watering trough, a dirt street, and a pile of manure. It had to be a western. It was a western, and on the sheriff's door was an enormous black-and-white poster: "Wanted Dead Or Alive, Jive James" (Americans call him Jesse). Santini introduced me to the director, Maurizio Lucidi, and arranged for me to stay on the set with my camera. He had to go back to Rome but would return to pick me up when the shooting stopped at six.

The director, who received his training cutting film for Orson Welles, speaks English, Spanish, Italian, French, and German. Very soon I was to learn why. When I explained my assignment, he lopped his arm over my shoulder, gave me a script of *The Greatest Robbery in the West*, and told me to talk to anyone and shoot any pictures I wanted. He said the movie was going to be great — a combination of *High Noon* and *Desperate Hours* — a sure sale to America and a natural for a television series. I went out behind the set with the script, a hunk of cheese, and an apple. Strange, choppy story, stranger dialogue. A sample of 1880 Italian Western conversation: "As soon as the guide comes, we cut out." Also, "We're doing our own thing."

When Lucidi asked me what I thought of the script, I told him I didn't know. Quickly he said, "Don't worry. We'll change it as we go along. You won't even recognize it when we're through."

I asked him why have any script, then?

"We need an idea of where we're going. Watch a few shots. You'll get the idea."

A scene was set up. The camera, the arc lights, and the reflectors were pointed at the porch of the general store. Leaning and sitting on the porch rail and steps were Erika Blank from Trieste, who speaks Italian; George Hilton from Uruguay, who speaks Spanish; Katia Christine from Holland, who speaks French; Walter Barnes, speaking German; and Hunt Powers, English.

As the reflectors were jockeyed to kill the shadows, Lucidi, who directs in Italian, shouted, "*Silenzio!*" Then "*Luci!*" The lights came on. "*Azione!*" The scene began.

The five different languages from five different actors were clanging and clashing together, sounding like a bad night at a dog pound. Nothing made any sense, but no one seemed to mind, and they kept going. Lucidi was everywhere, moving his hands up and down for loudness and softness, wide or narrow for length, and fanning his fingers and whipping his wrists for feeling. Later he joked, "Only an Italian, with Italian hands, can direct something like this."

Still later, at the projection room at Fono-Roma Dubbing Studio, I saw how it all came together. A cowboy was standing at a lighted podium, facing a screen showing a short scene that was "looped" so it could be played over and over again. At the side of the room, the dubbing director

was making last-minute changes in the script to accommo-
date the language. In the scene they were dubbing, a man
about to be shot was digging his own grave. In the script, the
gunman said, "O.K., half-breed, you'd better say your
prayers." Watching the film and following the script, the
director said it wasn't working. The lips on the screen were
still moving after the dialogue ended. He told the cowboy,
"Change the 'O.K.' to 'all right' and try a chuckle on the end.
Make it a long one." They tried it once, twice. The third
time, it was on the money. But for now, Lucidi, working
with a cast of five and with five different languages, was
doing what most directors could barely comprehend. After
the second take, which was a print, I asked him who would
be starred in the movie? He dropped his voice and led me
down to the end of the porch. "Actually, we have three
stars. In Germany, Walter Barnes gets top billing. He has a
big following up there. If the film goes to Spain, George
Hilton becomes the star. In America, it's Hunt Powers. It's
really up to the distributors; they decide who brings in the
public."

The porch scene ended, and the group scattered. It was
lunch-and-siesta time. The extras, stunt men, grips, and
workers had pasta, red wine, and cheese, and flaked out in
the shade with their hats over their eyes. A lighting
technician and I had a cup of coffee together. He told me,
"No one can keep an Italian quiet. I'm Italian, and I ought
to know. You've got to shoot with no sound." He recalled a
scene shot with sound, in which the cowboy and the leading
lady got on their horses to ride off into the sunset. At the
last minute, a group of extras and workers, who'd forgotten
about the microphones, leaped to their feet and began
cheering and applauding.

Hunt Powers joined us and began joking about the hard
facts of Roman movie-making. He told about a sensitive
American "method" actor who came over to play "mean-

ingful" roles. After learning his lines, and those of everyone else in his scenes, the actor was ready for the first day's shooting. It was a western. In his first scene, he was to rush into the colonel's office and describe a massacre. The colonel, played by one of the biggest stars in Rome, was supposed to calm him down, tell him that his wife was safe, and then give him instructions about how to protect the fort. The camera began rolling. The actor raced into the office, delivered his breathless report in fine dramatic style, and waited. The colonel, in full-dress uniform and standing before the American flag and a photograph of Abraham Lincoln, snapped to attention, looked him dead in the eye, and then, with gestures and facial movements ranging from sadness through matter-of-fact to rage, proceeded to count to twenty-five. Hunt talked on about Italian flesh-and-sex shots, about how they'd shot a scene the day before in which he spread his monk's robe out near a church altar and made love to an actress named Sonio Romanoff. He laughed. "That was for the Italian market. For the Spanish, they're talking about having me *rape her* on the altar." He went on about how Italy was tame compared to Spain, where there is no SPCA and horses are blow up on camera and their death throes filmed in extreme close-up and slow motion. He said a wounded gunman in Spain will writhe on camera for three and four minutes, flourishing a handful of bleeding scrap from the butcher shop, before the director decides to let him close his eyes and turn to the wall.

The sun was dropping, and a fresh breeze was rolling a paper cup down the wooden sidewalk in front of the saloon and flapping the "Jive James" poster on the sheriff's door. The limousine, with the chauffeur up front and Santini in the back, had parked in the shade of the church. I told Mr. Lucidi that I would like to come out the next day and the day after that, if possible. He shook my hand with both of his. "Wonderful! Wonderful! Anytime, just come on out and make yourself at home. But, one minute, before you go, I'd like to tell you something in confidence." Again, he steered me down the porch away from everyone. "Americans are wrong thinking we're just copying their westerns." He lowered his voice to keep the others from hearing. "What we're doing is adding the Italian concept of realism, call it neo-realism, to an old American myth, and it's working. Look at Jesse James. In your country, he's a saint. Over here we play him as a gangster. That's what he was. Europeans today are too sophisticated to believe in the honest gunman movie any more. They want the truth, and that's what we're giving them. Now, I don't want to be putting words in your mouth, but when you sit down to write this article, I hope you'll explain what we're trying to do over here, because a lot of us think it's very important. Do you have any questions? Anything? Anything I can help you on?"

I wanted to ask him if they were shooting the Spanish rape scene the next day in the morning or afternoon, but this wasn't the time for that. We shook hands again and agreed to have lunch.

I took a few shots of the saloon, the store, the "Jive James" poster, the crooked cross on top of the church, and climbed in the limo. Santini handed me a cold beer. "How'd it go?"

"Couldn't have been better." I tipped the beer at him. "Nice crowd. I'm coming back out tomorrow; there's something I want to see."

"O.K., I'll hang on to the limo and the driver. And tonight I'm going to take you to the finest restaurant in Italy. There'll be a lot of celebrities there."

I said, "Terrific," and sat back and sipped the beer. Then, "Santini, I'm sorry we couldn't work out the Crusade stuff. Maybe there's something else I can do."

His beer was in the drink holder, and he was skinning back the cellophane from a ten-inch cigar. He handed me one. "O.K., but not for me. For someone — shall we say — close to me. It's like this, I've got this girlfriend, and she's an actress. Maybe, somehow, you could work her into the article?"

I lit my cigar. I was way ahead of him. "What if I put her in *The Greatest Robbery in the West* story? Hell, maybe I can talk Lucidi into giving her a walk-on."

Santini beamed and slapped me on the leg. "Perfect, she'll love it." He sat with his feet up on the jump seat puffing his cigar, as we rolled along the tree-line Appian Way heading back for Rome. Then he closed his eyes. "You know, if you ever get tired of New York and L.A, I could use a good guy like you. Over here, you could make a bundle, you wouldn't have to break your ass, and you would have some fun doing it." He puffed again, and while the blue smoke was hanging in the air, he cut his eyes and slid over. "Hey, be sure and write it down. Fortunato, Angela Fortunato. That's F-O-R-T-U-N-A-T-O."